THE IN-SPECTRES CALL

The gym was filled with pu[illegible]
swimming and laughin[illegible]
PE teacher, Ms Legg, st[illegible]
open-mouthed. *I don't re*[illegible] *part of the display* . . . she thought.

'Look down there!' James pointed at the In-Spectres. They were staring up at the pupils floating past, pointing and giggling and poking each other in the ribs.

'Look – they're leaving!' hissed Lenny. The pair were now grinning and nodding to one another. The woman reached her hand up and waved her fingers slowly at James and Alexander. Her eyes flashed red as she mouthed 'Bye-bye!'

'That was *weird*!' James shuddered.

'James Simpson, master of understatement!' Alexander laughed nervously.

St Sebastian's School in Grimesford is the pits. No, really – it is.

Every year, the high school sinks a bit further into the boggy plague pit beneath it and, every year, the ghosts of the plague victims buried underneath it become a bit more cranky.

Egged on by their spooky ringleader, Edith Codd, they decide to get their own back – and they're willing to play dirty. *Really* dirty.

They kick up a stink by causing as much mischief as in inhumanly possible so as to get St Sebastian's closed down once and for all.

But what they haven't reckoned on is year-seven new boy, James Simpson and his friends Alexander and Lenny.

The question is, are the gang up to the challenge of laying St Sebastian's paranormal problem to rest, or will their school remain forever frightful?

There's only one way to find out . . .

The In-Spectres Call

B. STRANGE

EGMONT

Special thanks to:

Lynn Huggins-Cooper, St John's Walworth Church of England Primary School and Belmont Primary School

EGMONT

We bring stories to life

Published in Great Britain 2007
by Egmont UK Limited
239 Kensington High Street, London W8 6SA

Text by Lynn Huggins-Cooper
Illustrations by Pulsar Studio (Beehive Illustration)

ISBN 978 1 4052 3236 4

1 3 5 7 9 10 8 6 4 2

A CIP catalogue record for this title is available
from the British Library

Typeset by Avon DataSet Ltd, Bidford on Avon, Warwickshire
Printed and bound in Great Britain by the CPI Group

'More books – I love it!'
Ashley, age 11

'It's disgusting. . .'
Joe, age 10

'. . . it's all good!'
Alexander, age 9

'. . . loads of excitement and really gross!'
Jay, age 9

'I like the way there's the brainy boy, the brawny boy and the cool boy that form a team of friends'
Charlie, age 10

'That ghost Edith is wicked'
Matthew, age 11

'This is really good and funny!'
Sam, age 9

School versus . . .
Year-seven new boy
and chief spook-hunter
James Simpson
Headmaster's son
and official brainiac
Alexander Tick
Strong as an ox,
gentle as an
unusually tall lamb
Lenny Maxwell

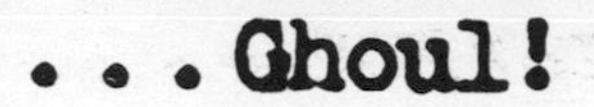

Loud-mouthed
ringleader of the
plague-pit ghosts

Edith Codd

Young ghost and
a secret wannabe
St Sebastian's pupil

William Scroggins

Bone idle ex-leech
merchant with a taste
for all things gross

Ambrose Harbottle

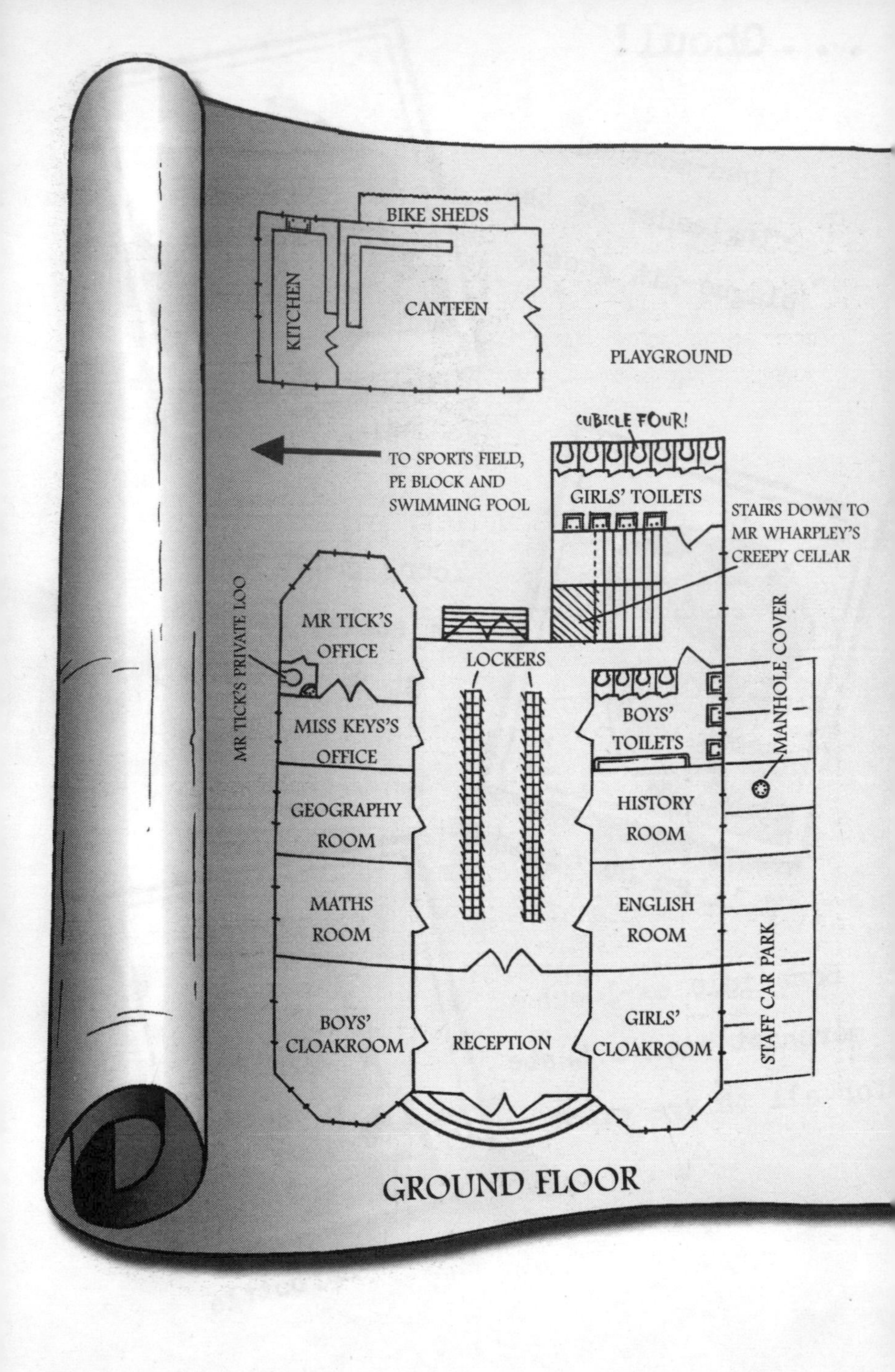
BIKE SHEDS
KITCHEN
CANTEEN
PLAYGROUND
CUBICLE FOUR!
TO SPORTS FIELD, PE BLOCK AND SWIMMING POOL
GIRLS' TOILETS
STAIRS DOWN TO MR WHARPLEY'S CREEPY CELLAR
MR TICK'S PRIVATE LOO
MR TICK'S OFFICE
LOCKERS
MANHOLE COVER
MISS KEYS'S OFFICE
BOYS' TOILETS
GEOGRAPHY ROOM
HISTORY ROOM
MATHS ROOM
ENGLISH ROOM
STAFF CAR PARK
BOYS' CLOAKROOM
RECEPTION
GIRLS' CLOAKROOM
GROUND FLOOR

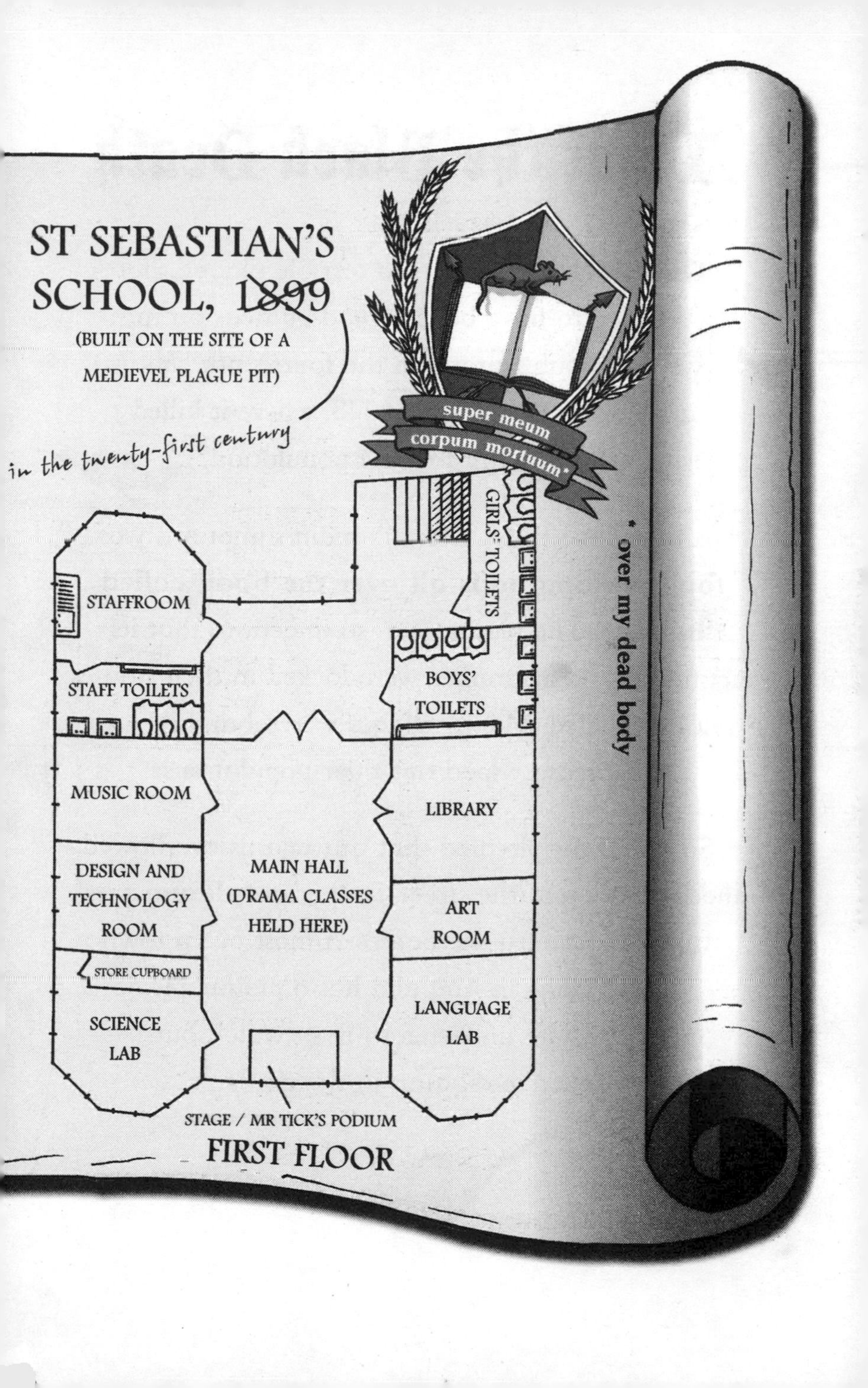
ST SEBASTIAN'S SCHOOL, 1899
(BUILT ON THE SITE OF A MEDIEVEL PLAGUE PIT)
in the twenty-first century
super meum corpum mortuum*
* over my dead body
GIRLS' TOILETS
STAFFROOM
STAFF TOILETS
BOYS' TOILETS
MUSIC ROOM
LIBRARY
DESIGN AND TECHNOLOGY ROOM
MAIN HALL (DRAMA CLASSES HELD HERE)
ART ROOM
STORE CUPBOARD
SCIENCE LAB
LANGUAGE LAB
STAGE / MR TICK'S PODIUM
FIRST FLOOR

About the Black Death

The Black Death was a terrible plague that is believed to have been spread by fleas on rats. It swept through Europe in the fourteenth century, arriving in England in 1348, where it killed over one third of the population.

One of the Black Death's main symptoms was **foul-smelling boils all over the body called 'buboes'**. The plague was so infectious that its victims and their families were locked in their houses until they died. Many villages were abandoned as the disease wiped out their populations.

So many people died that graveyards overflowed and bodies lay in the street, so special **'plague pits'** were dug to bury the bodies. Almost every town and village in England has a plague pit somewhere underneath it, so watch out when you're digging in the garden . . .

Dear Reader

As you may have already guessed, B. Strange is not a real name.

The author of this series is an ex-teacher who is currently employed by a little-known body called the Organisation For Spook Termination (Excluding Demons), or O.F.S.T.(E.D.). 'B. Strange' is the pen name chosen to protect his identity.

Together, we felt it was our duty to publish these books, in an attempt to save innocent lives. The stories are based on the author's experiences as an O.F.S.T.(E.D.) inspector in various schools over the past two decades.

Please read them carefully - you may regret it if you don't . . .

Yours sincerely
The Publisher.

PS - Should you wish to file a report on any suspicious supernatural occurrences at your school, visit **www.too-ghoul.com** and fill out the relevant form. We'll pass it on to O.F.S.T.(E.D.) for you.

PPS - All characters' names have been changed to protect the identity of the individuals. Any similarity to actual persons, living or undead, is purely coincidental.

CONTENTS

'What's that droning noise?' grumbled Edith Codd, leader of the plague-pit ghosts. She frowned and glared about the cavernous amphitheatre that had been built over the centuries in the sewers deep under St Sebastian's School.

Ambrose Harbottle, a leech merchant before the Black Death had carried him off over six hundred years earlier, was leaning against a stone pillar. He was humming a happy little ditty about 'juicy little leeches' to himself as he sorted through a tin of them. He popped one

in his mouth and chewed noisily, like a dog gnawing gristle.

'Shhh!' Edith hissed, scowling. '*Listen!*'

A loud voice was carrying down the pipes from the school above. 'It's that horrible headmaster,' she said. 'He thinks he's so incredibly important!'

'He's not the only one . . .' Ambrose whispered to William Scroggins, a young ghost who sat at his feet. William choked back a giggle.

'He's such a bore! I can't think *why* he imagines anyone wants to listen to him . . .' Edith went on, shaking her head.

Ambrose nudged William and smirked. William spluttered.

'He's so full of his own importance – he's like a puffed-up town crier!' grumbled Edith.

'Takes one to know one,' Ambrose muttered. William sniggered.

'It's bad enough having to put up with those horrible children laughing and shouting all day,' moaned Edith. William smiled wistfully at the thought of the fun the pupils were having, 'without that idiot droning on and on!'

She stopped suddenly, frozen in place like a stoat scenting a particularly delicious rabbit. Her large nostrils flared and her eyes narrowed.

'What was that . . .? A visit from the *who* . . .?' she hissed. She pressed her ear up against the rusty pipe.

A small spider gasped, screwed up its face, spat and ran away as a waft of Edith's breath hit it.

Up in the school, high above the ghosts, Mr Tick the headmaster was in St Sebastian's staffroom, trying hard to get the attention of the assembled teachers. They lay slumped in their chairs, sipping coffee.

'Listen, everybody!' Mr Tick demanded, clapping his hands. 'We are having a visit from the school inspectors this afternoon. There is, of course, nothing for *most* of us to worry about. May I remind you that the inspectors will be listing the strengths and weaknesses of the school during their visit. The last time they came, they noted a lack of care and guidance from some of

the teaching staff. Can't possibly see how they got that idea, ha, ha! I will, of course, be showing them round all the new facilities personally, and Miss Keys shall serve them tea in my beautifully decorated office –'

'Won't they want to talk to the children, too?' asked Ms Legg, the PE teacher.

'Why on *earth* would they want to do th–
I mean, no, I shouldn't think so – busy people
and all that . . .'

Edith pressed her ear against the pipe. 'A visit from the In-Spectres? That sounds interesting . . .' whispered Edith to herself. 'It sounds very *official* . . .'

'I remember the last report,' Mr Watts, the science teacher, grumbled. 'I seem to recall that school leadership and management weren't seen as too hot either –'

'I don't remember any such thing,' harrumphed Mr Tick. 'You must have misread the report . . . Anyway – right! That's settled then. Everyone must be on the look-out for visitors with clipboards. I shall be accompanying them round, of course . . .'

Edith could *hear* the man smiling, his voice was so smarmy.

'We always know when there are visitors in school,' a female voice said quietly. Edith strained to hear. 'We actually get to *see* the headmaster in the classrooms for once . . .'

Edith jumped backwards as a hoot of laughter that suddenly changed to a coughing fit rumbled down the pipes.

'I heard that!' the headmaster growled. 'Look – the bottom line is this: we must all pull together to convince the inspectors that we have a smooth-running school filled with caring teachers and happy pupils, or St Sebastian's will close. I don't think anybody here wants to be out of a job, do they?' Edith could hear rustling, as though people were shuffling about in their seats. 'No. Funny that – I didn't think so. There aren't too many jobs in Grimesford, unless you count the glue factory, and I don't think they're hiring. So it's up to you lot.'

Edith heard heavy footsteps as someone stalked out of the room. She heard the doors swish and then a murmuring as people started to talk.

'Well, I'm not looking forward to it, I must say! Those people breathing down your neck. What do they know about life in the raw, at the chalkface . . .?'

'At least it'll keep old Tricky Ticky on his toes!' a voice laughed.

'I get nervous when I'm being watched . . . I set fire to my tie in the lab by accident last time . . .'

Edith jumped up, hugging herself with excitement.

'This is great news!' she giggled. The words sounded wrong coming from Edith's thin lips. William shuddered. 'These In-Spectres have got the teachers and that horrid headmaster rattled, so they *must* be a good thing! There was me thinking the man was totally useless, then he comes up with something that could sink St Sebastian's for good! Oh, happy days!'

CHAPTER 2
A BIG ANNOUNCEMENT

Mr Tick stood on the stage in the hall. His arms were behind his back and his chin pointed proudly in the air.

Ooh . . . he looks just like a sergeant major, stood there . . . Miss Keys, the school secretary, thought to herself. She sighed and leaned back in her chair. The swelling music from the CD player at the back added to her enjoyment, and from time to time she sighed happily again. The rest of the staff sat waiting for assembly to begin. Mr Watts glared at James Simpson and Lenny

Maxwell as their line of year sevens walked into the hall.

'Blimey! We haven't even done anything – yet!' whispered James.

Lenny tittered, and Alexander Tick poked James in the back.

'Shhh! Dad's about to make an announcement!' Alexander breathed quietly.

The pupils sat down in a rumble of shuffling. Mr Tick raised his hands in front of him, waiting for everyone to be quiet.

'He looks like he's pushing an invisible trolley – tea anyone?' James muttered.

Alexander scowled at him.

'If everyone is *quite* ready – and that means *you*, James Simpson. I'm watching you, boy . . .' said Mr Tick, frowning directly at James. 'I have some very exciting news!'

'St Sebastian's is closing down and a theme park for pupils opening in its place?' Lenny whispered.

James stifled a snort.

'The school inspectors are arriving this afternoon!' Mr Tick continued with a huge smile, clapping his hands together.

'Great. Can't wait. Super,' James said under his breath.

'They will, of course, be looking at school improvement. As you know, our drive for excellence at St Sebastian's never stops. It is our duty, as teachers, to make sure the inspectors take note of this.' He smiled at the teachers sat behind him. They fidgeted and shifted uncomfortably. 'It is your duty, as pupils,' he said, sweeping his hand in an arc to include all of the children assembled in front of him, 'to be shining examples of the best that St Sebastian's has to offer!'

Alexander beamed at his father. A shaft of sunlight struggled through the grimy windows behind the headmaster, surrounding him with a glowing halo. Alexander sighed.

James nudged Lenny. 'Look at Stick!' he whispered. 'He's like one of those soppy children on an old-fashioned birthday card – the ones with huge, shiny eyes!'

Lenny smirked. 'Poor old Stick!' he murmured, trying to be sympathetic to his friend Alexander. He wrestled with his lips, hoping to stifle a smile, but his lips won. He grinned, shaking his head.

'Remember, St Sebastian's is only as good as its staff and pupils,' said Mr Tick.

'Poor old St Sebastian's – we're doomed!' whispered James, rolling his eyes.

Mr Tick finished, smiling broadly. 'So it is up to *you* to show the inspectors the *true value* of this school!'

'About twenty-five pence?' whispered Lenny.

James honked with laughter.

Mr Watts leapt up and rushed towards him.

James's eyes widened. Lenny shoved a huge hankie into his hand. James started to scrub at his face.

'Sorry, sir – hay fever . . . erm . . . asthma!' he explained. 'May I be excused? I must get my inhaler . . .' James stumbled along the line, treading on toes and tripping over feet.

Lenny looked horrified. Everyone turned to look at James as he left the hall. Mr Tick's face was purple with rage.

'I will not allow any bad behaviour to spoil this visit. Any pupil who sees himself as a *comedian* –' he stared after James – 'will find themselves in hot water. *Very* hot water indeed. Be warned.' He glared around the hall, catching the eyes of pupils he suspected of bad behaviour.

Alexander shifted uncomfortably. He hung his head and looked at the floor. His dad had an annoying knack of making him feel guilty for no reason.

'Right – you are dismissed!' Mr Tick said, sharply.

Alexander felt as though his dad was speaking directly to him. He trudged out of the hall and back to his form room. James was waiting there for him.

'Sorry,' he said, giving him a friendly punch on the arm.

'Whatever,' Alexander mumbled, packing his bag for first lesson. He turned and walked away.

'Aw, Stick, I didn't mean anything by it,' James called after him.

Lenny frowned. 'Just leave him for now. He'll come round.' he sighed.

'I know I took it a bit far, but does Mr Tick really believe all that stuff about the school being great? I *know* teachers live on another planet, but surely he can see what a dump this is?' James picked a flake of grey paint off the wall and watched it float to the floor. 'So the inspectors will be able to see that too, whatever we do, right?'

'Well, we'll soon see,' replied Lenny. 'They'll be here soon, so they can make their own minds up . . .'

CHAPTER 3
VIP (VERY IMPORTANT PLAN)

The amphitheatre in the sewers was full of ghosts milling about and chatting. Edith had called yet *another* meeting. Candles poked into skulls flickered on the walls and Bertram Ruttle, a ghoulish musician, played a gently haunting tune on his ribcage xylophone. Ambrose and Lady Grimes, spooky sweethearts, danced happily to the music.

'Right, everybody – settle down now. This is important!' announced Edith.

'Isn't it always?' drawled the Headless Horseman to a little ghost by his side. She giggled.

Ambrose and Lady Grimes seated themselves on a bench made from a pile of bones.

Edith banged on the upturned barrel she used as her dressing table and ranting point. A spider that had been dozing in a crack scowled at her and walked away on eight wobbly legs. 'I have some very important news! The school is being visited by the In-Spectres.'

She crossed her arms and smiled around at everyone as though she had given them a treat.

Ambrose stared into the distance, picking absent-mindedly at a crusty scab on his chin. He popped it into his mouth and started to crunch.

'Ambrose! This is *important*! Pay attention!' Edith shouted.

Ambrose tumbled over backwards, falling off the bench with his legs waving in the air. He jumped up quickly, helped by Lady Grimes.

'Sorry, Edith!' he mumbled.

'Well, then – what did I say?' Edith asked.

'Erm . . . it was about . . . maybe we should . . . it was very important . . .' Ambrose scratched his head and shuffled from foot to foot.

'We're really interested to hear more about these In-Spectres who are visiting the school, aren't we, Ambrose?' William piped up.

Ambrose patted the boy's head and smiled. He took a deep breath. 'Of course we are, William. As I was just saying, who are these In-Spectres, Edith?'

'Specs? Are these peddlers of spectacles?' asked Lady Grimes, smoothing down her beautiful clothes. She had been a wealthy woman when she was alive, and she was still dressed in the remnants of velvet and furs.

'Ooh – it could be, my dear!' Ambrose beamed. 'You are *so* very clever!'

Lady Grimes fluttered her eyelashes.

'Of course it's not!' Edith shouted. 'They are –'

'Are they some sort of audience? You know, inspect–, erm, spectators? Like when you go to watch the dancing bears? Ooh, I love big, cuddly dancing bears . . . and I could play them a tune or two!' said Bertram Ruttle, picking out another tune on his bony xylophone.

'For goodness' *sake*! Can I get a word in edgeways? Don't be so ridiculous!' spat Edith. 'Shut up, all of you! If you would just *listen* for a moment!' she yelled. Her eyes were wild, and specks of spittle flew from her lips.

'Sorry, Edith,' muttered Bertram.

The ghosts shuffled and fidgeted, trying to avoid Edith's glare.

'You tell us, Edith,' coaxed Ambrose. 'What are these In-Spectres coming to do?'

Edith took a deep breath and flared her nostrils.

'Well . . . er . . . they are very important visitors,' she said. She frowned. She started to fidget too, and smoothed down her wiry, red hair. A flurry of dandruff flakes drifted down and settled on William, like a sprinkling of snow.

'Why are they very important, Edith?' asked William, shaking his shoulders. The flakes wafted down and caught in a spider's web.

'You know . . . important visitors . . . important because . . . well . . . everybody has to fuss about to get ready for their visit – like a visit from the king!' Edith didn't *really* know who the inspectors were, but she could sniff out an opportunity to cause trouble for St Sebastian's a mile off.

Lady Grimes leapt up and started brushing down the folds of her dress again.

'The king! I must look my best!' She started to smooth down her hair and pinch her cheeks in an effort to make them pink.

Ambrose began to cough. The leech he'd been chewing shot out of his mouth and plopped on to Edith's barrel, crawling off quickly.

'I remember when the king visited our village,' an elderly ghost murmured. 'He was on a Royal Progress through the countryside and all the maidens put on their best gowns, hoping he'd notice them, but of course he only had eyes for gentlewomen, like our lovely Lady Grimes, here.' He cracked a toothless grin.

Lady Grimes lowered her eyes shyly.

'Ah, those were the days. They even renamed the local inn "The King's Head" after his visit.' The old man smiled.

'How *original*!' Edith sneered. 'Can we get back to the matter in hand, please?' she said, sharply, glaring at the ghosts in front of her.

The old ghost sank back into his seat and shut his eyes, dozing off again. Many of the other phantoms were looking at one another, raising their eyebrows and talking excitedly about a visit from the king.

'It's not *actually* the king . . . oh, give me *strength*! I was just trying to make you understand how important the visitors are!'

'It'll be exciting for the children,' Ambrose muttered, picking a lump of black sludge from between his teeth.

'What?' shouted Edith pushing her face close to Ambrose's.

'You know, meeting the king and all that . . .' he smiled vaguely.

Edith sighed deeply, blowing rancid breath across Ambrose's face. He winced and looked puzzled.

'Ambrose. It. Is. Not. *Actually*. The King! It is a visit from very important people *like* the king. Oh, never mind! The point is, this visit is perfect for our campaign!'

Ambrose frowned. 'Campaign?' he mouthed at William.

William shrugged. The elderly ghost woke up again.

'Campaign? Oh, yes. I remember a campaign when we marched for king and country! We were bold, we were brave –'

'Shut *up*!' roared Edith. The old ghost faded suddenly with fright. 'Our campaign to get rid of those awful children, of course!' Edith went on. 'We have a chance to have peace at last – no

more trampling feet, no more *laughing*!' She shuddered. 'We can be rid of them forever!'

She threw her head back and cackled, an evil gleam in her eye.

'These In-Spectres will look at the way things work at the school,' continued Edith slowly, as though she was explaining something to somebody very stupid. 'These people have the power to close the school down permanently!' she shrieked. 'If we mess up St Sebastian's they won't like what they see and the school will get a bad report!'

The amphitheatre was suddenly silent. Ambrose shifted uncomfortably. William's eyes were wide. What did Edith want them to do now?

CHAPTER 4
THE COUNTDOWN BEGINS . . .

Mr Tick marched up the corridor, his head turning from side to side as he examined the school before the inspectors arrived. His expensive leather shoes clicked on the wooden floor and he smiled to himself.

He paused in front of his office door and buffed the already gleaming brass plate with his hankie. It shone at him and showed him the reflection of a man meant to be in charge – or so he thought. He brushed his hair back out of his eyes and checked his teeth.

Oh, Richard . . . sometimes you are just too fabulous for words! he thought, as he admired his reflection. He frowned as he found a grey hair and tugged it out. Looking at it with disgust, he flung it on the floor. He ground it under the heel of one of his shiny Italian shoes, and swept off to reception. There he admired the huge bunch of perfect roses in a vase on the table. Spoiling the scene was a small boy sitting on a nearby chair, looking rather green.

'You, boy! Why aren't you in lessons?' Mr Tick thundered. He liked to make pupils jump.

The pupil did just that. 'Sorry, sir. I'm waiting for my mum, sir. I'm going home because I feel sick.'

'Sick? As in vomit?' The headmaster drew back and glared at the child. He wrinkled his nose and fluttered his fingers at the boy as though he was shooing away an annoying insect. 'Get yourself to Miss Keys's office! We can't have you cluttering up this beautiful reception area!'

'But, sir, I feel sicker when I move about, and Miss Keys told me to wait here because it would be easier for my mum. I feel really, really ill –'

'Never mind that, boy! Run along! I can't have a *pupil* being the first thing the inspectors see when they come in! And especially not a sickly little specimen like you! Now, do as you are told – go away!'

The boy scuttled off, whimpering and hiccupping to himself. He dashed into the toilets and Mr Tick shuddered as he heard the sound of violent retching. Glancing around the perfect, pupil-free reception, he carried on with his own school inspection.

The floors gleamed and were unusually free of litter. Down the corridor in front of him, Mr Wharpley, the caretaker, was leaning on a broom and staring out of the window.

'Mr Wharpley!' the headmaster shouted. The caretaker jumped, sending his broom flying with a clatter. 'I've done my best, headmaster. It's those flaming kids –'

'No – I was going to say you've done a good job for once, Mr Wharpley. Keep it up!' He sailed past the caretaker, leaving him open-mouthed.

Praise? From the headmaster? What is the world coming to? thought Mr Wharpley, picking up his broom.

Mr Tick marched across the playground and through the boys' changing room in the PE block. There was a faint smell of sweat masked with bleach. He wandered over to the door and checked for any signs of mud trailing in from the sports field, but found none. He smiled happily. He stuck his head into each toilet cubicle to check they were spotless and ready for the inspectors.

'All clean . . . marvellous. Urgh! Good grief! What *is* that terrible smell?' Mr Tick gasped, pulling a crisp, white hankie from his pocket and

holding it over his nose. The toilets looked clean; the sinks were shiny and the floor was spotless. They didn't *smell* clean though. He coughed. There was a dreadful whiff, like old, curdled milk mixed with dead rat. What on *earth* had Wharpley been using as toilet cleaner? *Eau de Rodent?*

Mr Tick flew to the girls' changing room and tugged open the doors to the toilets there. He retched as he breathed in the same awful stench.

A year-eight girl came out of one of the cubicles and screeched as she saw the headmaster. Mr Tick ignored her and let the main door go with a bang on his way out.

'Wharpley! *Wharpley!*' he roared.

In the science lab, a nervous year-seven pupil heard the noise and dropped a set of test tubes in surprise. He yelped as a cloud of blue smoke filled the air. Across the playground in the kitchen, Lynn Cooper, one of the dinner ladies, sniffed sharply and crossed her arms. 'Look lively, Sue – His Lordship is on the warpath again! Better get on. I was enjoying that coffee break as well . . .' She put down her cup and crammed the rest of her chocolate biscuit into her mouth.

'When isn't he on the warpath, pet?' grumbled Sue. 'There's always *something* for him to moan about . . .'

Mr Tick stormed back to his office. He pushed open the door and yelled an order.

'Miss Keys! Call Mr Wharpley *immediately*! There's not a moment to lose!' he bellowed.

Miss Keys dropped her pen and jumped out of her chair. She called the caretaker on his walkie-talkie. It crackled and buzzed and she started to tap her nails on the desk anxiously. Mr Tick leant on her desk, watching her with narrowed eyes.

'Mr Wharpley! Come in, *please*! It's an emergency!' she begged.

The walkie-talkie finally crackled into life. Miss Keys took a deep breath to steady herself.

'I'm *here*, Miss Keys! Don't get yourself all worked up! Don't say I need the sick bucket and sawdust again! I've only just finished cleaning out one set of toilets that some horrible little oik threw up in – or should I say *on*? A year seven it was, whimpering about his mother coming to collect him. These flaming kids – they really know how to spoil a perfectly nice school . . .' Mr Wharpley ranted on.

'Mr Tick needs you – and he wants you to come straight away, Mr Wharpley!' Miss Keys

ged. She listened, then breathed a sigh of relief. He was on his way. She peeped up at Mr Tick through her fringe.

'Shall I make you a nice soothing cup of coffee, sir?' she asked.

Mr Tick sighed. 'That would be wonderful, Miss Keys – you are a treasure indeed!' he smarmed, going through into his office.

Miss Keys blushed. *I'll make him a cup of coffee just as he likes it!* she thought.

Mr Wharpley burst into the office, pushing his cleaning trolley in front of him.

'Where is it? I'm ready!' he said, armed with a bottle of spray cleaner and a damp cloth.

'Mr Tick wants you to go straight in, Mr Wharpley,' said Miss Keys. He raised his eyebrows.

'Has Mr Tick been sick?' he asked.

'Nobody's been sick, Mr Wharpley,' Miss Keys sighed.

The caretaker shrugged, rapped on the door and went in.

'Ah – Mr Wharpley. All the toilets smell like something has crawled in and died in them. Any explanations?' said Mr Tick in a clipped voice.

The caretaker's mouth dropped open.

'It's not hard. What on earth have you been using to clean them?'

'I-I used *Fragrance of Flowers – the flowery fragrance for your loo*, same as always! I buy those industrial-sized drums and –'

'Never mind that now, man! This is an emergency! The inspectors are due any minute. The toilets stink. Sort it out. Put a toilet freshener in every cubicle immediately!'

'But I did!' Mr Wharpley looked confused.

'Obviously not! Do it now! Come on, man! Don't hang about! Chop, chop!'

Mr Tick bustled the caretaker out of the room and he shot down to the supply cupboard in his

cellar. He filled his bucket with container after container of sickly pink *Fragrance of Flowers* and rushed off to carry out Operation De-stench.

'I don't understand *why* there's a smell, but there won't be for long! I'm not going to give those inspectors an excuse to get rid of Reg Wharpley, oh, no!'

Mr Tick closed his eyes and took a deep breath to steady himself. He reached out and felt along the back of his chair for his best tie – but it wasn't there. He rummaged in his desk, but couldn't find it. He frowned. A tin of chocolate biscuits with the label 'You deserve the best!' jostled for space with a tub of hair wax, a nose-hair trimmer and several sets of golf-themed cufflinks – but no tie. He heaved open the heavy bottom drawer. It was lined with official papers from the education department, and held his spare pair of shiny Italian leather shoes and the briefcase Miss Keys had given him for his last birthday. He liked to look smart on his visits to the town hall. Hmmm . . . still no tie. He pressed the intercom button.

'Miss Keys! Come in here, please!' he called.

The secretary bustled in, smiling and patting her hair. 'How may I help, sir?' she trilled.

'My tie. It was here ten minutes ago and now it's gone. I can see my *second* best tie, but I wanted my *best* tie – the blue silk one with the golf club crests on it. Have you moved it?'

'No, sir!' the secretary gasped, her hand flying up to flutter at her throat. 'I wouldn't dream of it – not without asking! I sent your jacket to the cleaner's last week like you asked me, but I'd never do anything without asking permission, sir!'

'I should think not.' Mr Tick sighed. He picked up his second best tie – the grey silk one with thin red stripes. He picked off some imaginary fluff and held it out towards the secretary. 'This will have to do. Miss Keys, will you do the honours?'

Miss Keys took the tie. She paused, her cheeks flushing pink.

'Miss Keys! Time *is* of the essence!' the headmaster snapped.

Miss Keys gave a little squeak and a jump, and tied a neat knot in the tie.

'There you go, sir – nice and smart!' she sighed, patting the knot and stepping back.

'And ready for action!' Mr Tick said putting his fists up like a boxer.

Miss Keys watched Mr Tick as he left the room. *My hero!* she thought.

CHAPTER 5
A WHIFF OF TROUBLE

'Right – we'd better get ourselves to first lesson. The teachers are all on the warpath today!' said James.

'Dad's been really worried,' said Alexander. 'He says his job's on the line if anything goes wrong. They could even close the school!'

'Don't worry, Stick. I'm sure it'll be fine,' said Lenny, patting his friend's arm.

They rushed on down the corridor. James skidded to a halt outside the boys' toilets. Lenny and Alexander banged into the back of him.

'Can you smell that?' James groaned. 'Hey – perhaps Gordon 'The Gorilla' Carver has a dodgy belly!' He wafted his hand backwards and forwards in front of his face, smirking at the thought of the school bully with a funny tummy. 'I can't think of anything else that would smell that awful!' he choked.

'I can,' said Alexander. His eyes widened. Slowly, it dawned on James and Lenny what their friend was thinking. 'What if it's those ghosts from the plague pit under the school again?' whispered Alexander.

The boys stared at the toilet door in silence.

'Well, whatever it is, have to take a look,' James said.

Alexander's eyes widened further still with fear. 'But what if . . .?' he whispered.

'We *have* to look. We need to know what's going on. It might be nothing!' James smiled. 'Let's stick our heads round the door on a count

of three and have a look. We don't even need to go in if you don't want to.' He raised his eyebrows and smiled again encouragingly.

'I don't know, James,' Lenny protested. 'We'll be late for PE, and Ms Legg will be really mad. What if we come in late and the inspectors are there already? We'll be in big trouble!' he fretted.

James put a hand on each friend's shoulder. 'It's down to us, guys . . . we can't walk away from this. It could be important. The inspectors are coming today, so we don't want any funny business. St Sebastian's might be a rubbish school – but it's ours. We can't let some ghosts get it shut down!'

'You're right, James. We need to protect the school,' Alexander sighed. 'Just a look though. I'm not going in there.'

James grinned. 'I *knew* I could count on you two!' He laughed. 'OK . . . one . . .' Alexander tried to breathe deeply. 'Two . . .' James rested

his hand on the door handle. 'Wow, it's really cold!' he whispered. He pulled his hand back for a moment and they could see frost crystals gleaming on it. He put his hand back and grabbed the handle sharply. 'Three!' James flung the door open and looked inside. 'Well, it looks norm–'

He stepped into the toilets and his foot crunched something brittle.

'*Phwoar*! What a whiff!' James honked, covering his nose with his hand.

Lenny and Alexander looked over his shoulder. They could see containers of bright-pink toilet freshener smashed all over the tiled floor.

'Dad'll go *mad* if he sees this!' Alexander breathed.

Alexander and Lenny stepped into the toilet. Sticky pink goo was smeared over the tiles and crushed freshener was crammed into all the plugholes.

'Wow!' exclaimed Lenny. The air was heavy with a sickening mixture of perfume and *bad* things.

'Do you think it might be a miasma – a cloud left over from some kind of awful illness?' Alexander asked, coughing.

'But – what about the toilet fresheners? Who's smashed all these?' James kicked a chunk of pink goo. 'Even The Gorilla's not *that* stupid!' he said.

'Well, maybe . . . maybe they blew about! It *is* rather windy in here . . .' Alexander looked around, trying to see if there was a window open.

'Yeah, you'd expect there to be *wind* in a toilet, if you know what I mean . . . but none of the windows or doors is open!' James felt around the window frames. 'No draught either – maybe Mr Wharpley painted them shut so he'd save himself the job of making sure they're closed every night!'

'Stick, your hair's flapping about!' Lenny whispered.

Just then, the front of his blazer flapped in the breeze. Gusts of wind seemed to push and tug at the boys, yanking their ties and messing their hair.

'What is it?' Alexander hissed. 'What's going on?'

'I don't know, but we're going to find out!' James said, gritting his teeth. He marched down the room, pulling each cubicle door open in turn. 'Nothing's there. Blimey! The smell's even worse in this one!' he choked.

Lenny and Alexander stepped close behind him to peer into the cubicle. The smell was so strong it made their eyes water. The wind howled higher.

'This is weird. It's like we're caught in some kind of spectral vortex . . .' said Alexander.

The wind swirled around them, picking up sheets of toilet paper and pieces of toilet freshener. It whirled scented grit into the boys' faces.

'A *what*?' shouted James above the moaning wind. He scrubbed at his eyes.

'A vortex – a column of air, like a tornado. You know, a twister –' said Alexander.

'Never mind what it's called, or what it's like – I think we should get out of here!' shouted

Lenny. He ducked his head as a toilet brush swept past, showering him with sticky liquid.

The boys held on to each other and struggled towards the door. Out in the corridor, on the other side of the door, everything was calm. Not a poster on the wall was flapping. James pulled Lenny and Lenny pushed Alexander. They pulled their way through the tornado slowly, grabbing hold of pipes and basins.

'Nearly there!' shouted James. 'Keep it up!'

Suddenly, the main door slammed shut with a crack. The wind moaned on and rattled the door, mocking the boys.

They were trapped.

CHAPTER 6
THE ONLY WAY IS UP

Edith looked out across the amphitheatre at the assembled ghosts. *What a motley crew . . .* she thought. *Still, they're all I have, so they'll have to do!* She straightened her shoulders.

'My colleagues! This is a call to arms!' she shouted. 'We must crowd into the school and create a wave of havoc! Fear, confusion and terror must be our watchwords!' she roared. Ghosts shuffled from foot to foot, gazing around the roof of the amphitheatre. None of them wanted to catch Edith's eye. William sighed.

'Not again, Ambrose. I can't bear it. There's always some stupid scheme or other. Why can't Edith settle down and be happy? I don't want to cause trouble in the school. I love the kids with all their laughter and noise. It's like having real friends,' he moaned quietly. 'No offence, Ambrose!' he added quickly, looking up at him.

'None taken! A lad needs pals his own age. Chin up, son! I'm sure it won't be as bad as all that,' smiled Ambrose.

Edith, up at the front, carried on ranting. She was enjoying herself thoroughly.

'We must behave like wild poltergeists!' she yelled, throwing a skull across the room. It bounced off the wall and landed with a 'plop' on the Headless Horseman's shoulders. The jaw clacked open and shut a few times.

'Hey – I'm back in business!' the no longer Headless Horseman joked, making the skull move as he talked.

Edith scowled and carried on. 'We must hurl books round the library and classrooms! We must tear out pages and throw them around in a hail of mess! Make the library look like a rubbish tip!'

'Most of the books are rubbish anyway!' whispered Ambrose. William smiled thinly. Ambrose nudged him and grinned. 'Cheer up!'

By now, Edith was waving her arms wildly and her eyes gleamed.

'Empty the dustbins and whisk the rubbish along the corridors. We shall make a terrible mess and anger the In-Spectres!' She threw her head back and cackled. 'Scrape the desks and draw rude pictures of the teachers! We all need to work as a team, bent on destruction!'

'I think she's lost in a world of her own, that one . . .' Ambrose grumbled. 'Rude pictures indeed!'

He held up a scrap of toilet paper he'd been doodling on with sludge while Edith spoke. On it there was a drawing of Edith with a long scrawny neck and wild hair, waving her arms in the air. Drops of spittle were flying from her mouth. She was very skinny but had a huge, wobbly bottom.

'Rude enough, lad?' Ambrose whispered, his eyes twinkling with mischief. William giggled.

'What's that?' roared Edith, as she caught sight of the piece of paper. She swept across the amphitheatre, her hand held out in front of her.

William dropped the paper in fright, but Lady Grimes whisked it up. With a few strokes of sludge she transformed the picture into an elegant drawing of Edith. The fat bottom was changed into a beautiful silk bustle.

'Look, Edith. Ambrose drew you. Isn't he clever?' smiled Lady Grimes. Edith snatched the paper from her and her mouth dropped open.

'It's . . . it's *lovely*!' She beamed at Ambrose, flashing her crumbling brown teeth. 'Ambrose, I had no idea you were so artistic!'

William hid a grin behind his hand.

Edith and made her way back to the front of the amphitheatre clutching the drawing. 'I know we shall all work together to make this campaign work. Ambrose is setting us all a fine example of cooperation!'

Ambrose shrugged and gave a wobbly smile. 'Thank you, my lovely!' he whispered in Lady Grimes's ear.

She smiled at him so sweetly that he forgot where he was.

'Together, we shall do everything it takes to anger the In-Spectres, so that they realise what a bad school St Sebastian's is and force it to close!' said Edith, squirming with excitement.

Both Ambrose and William frowned and shuddered.

'I myself have given us all a head start, of course,' Edith said proudly, patting her hair. 'I crept into that stupid headmaster's study and hid his favourite tie. Won't he be surprised when he sees it blocking his private toilet!' she cackled with pleasure. Several ghosts laughed politely and were rewarded by one of Edith's awful smiles. 'He's so vain, so keen on preening – I really hit him where it hurts!' She smashed her fist down hard on the barrel. A metal hoop pinged off it and hit the skull the Headless Horseman was still playing with, completely shattering it . The headless ghost took his *real* head from under his arm and held it up.

'Steady on, old girl!' the head called.

'Sor*ry*,' said Edith, spoiling her apology by rolling her eyes at the same time.

'Anyway, back to the matter in hand. Next, I went into the toilets and smashed up all of the smelly perfume pomanders. Disgusting things – they smell like the tussie-mussies, those silly bunches of flowers we used to carry to ward off the plague. We all know how useless they are, don't we? We're the living – or rather, the dead – proof of that!'

All round the amphitheatre, ghosts nodded sadly in agreement.

'They were about as useful as being bled by leeches!' a voice came from the back.

Ambrose spun round crossly but couldn't see who had been talking. He pulled a pouch from his pocket and stroked a fat leech that was poking a slimy head out of the top.

'Don't listen, my pretty!' he murmured.

'Anyway, while you're all engaged as foot soldiers, Ambrose and I shall be awaiting the arrival of the In-Spectres themselves in the entrance hall. I should think they shall want to meet *all* of the most important people attached to the school – and that, of course, includes me. Oh, yes, and Ambrose,' she added.

Ambrose jumped up, startled.

'Why me?' he croaked.

'Because, my dear, you are terribly important and clever,' said Lady Grimes, tickling his cheek.

Ambrose took a deep breath and looked calmer.

'You know, I rather think she has her eye on you, and why not? You're a fine figure of a man!' smiled Lady Grimes. 'And she seemed rather impressed by your, er, beautiful drawing of her . . .'

Ambrose slapped his forehead in disgust and pulled a face.

'Yuck! What have I done? I'd hate her to think I fancied her – blah!'

Edith was beaming around at the assembled ghosts, waiting for somebody to ask her more about her very important plan. The ghosts shuffled and wandered around the amphitheatre, talking in small groups. The Headless Horseman galloped off to carry out his task. His horse's hooves made sparks on the ground as they clattered against the stone. Bertram Ruttle collected a group of ghosts to haunt the staffroom with ghostly music. He played a tune on his bone xylophone and they marched along behind him. A small ghost played castanets made from hip bones, and a tall thin ghost played a saxophone carved from a chunky spine. William sighed, sadly.

'Don't worry, lad! Remember what I said – it'll be fine.' Ambrose patted William's head, kissed Lady Grimes and took a deep breath before he trotted across to Edith's side.

'Come along, William!' smiled Lady Grimes. 'We shall go together. I'm sure we shall be able to scupper Edith's plans – both her plans for the school and her plans for Ambrose!' She held out her hand and William slipped his skinny fingers into hers. 'As long as Edith doesn't realise what we're up to, of course!' she added.

William peeped at Edith. She was telling Ambrose again about her plans, her arms waving in the air wildly. Ambrose was nodding, looking round and scratching his bottom. William grinned, then he and Lady Grimes began their journey to the land above.

'Mr Tick, sir! Sorry to bother you when you're so busy . . .' Miss Keys gushed. Her cheeks were pink and her eyes shone with nervous excitement. 'The inspectors are here, sir! I thought you'd want to know straight away.'

Mr Tick quickly saved the game of solitaire he was playing and switched to his 'St Sebastian's – A First Class Education!' screensaver. He smirked. He liked the play on words and had convinced himself it was his idea, even though Alexander had thought of it.

'Very good, Miss Keys,' he said. 'I shall go down to meet our very important guests!' He stood up and straightened his already straight tie. Stopping briefly to examine his hair in the shiny brass nameplate on his door, he rushed back to his desk for more hair wax. He ran his fingers through his hair and slicked down his eyebrows with his waxy fingers.

'Will I do, Miss Keys?' he smarmed.

'Oh, *yes*, headmaster!' she sighed. 'You're perfect!'

Mr Tick beamed, then swept off down the main corridor towards reception. Waiting for him were two smart people in dark suits. They were facing away from him, clutching clipboards that screamed the message 'I am *VERY* important!' to anyone looking. The woman was tall and thin with short hair in a neat, efficient style. The man was slightly shorter and broad shouldered. His shoes were very, very shiny. Mr Tick felt quite jealous.

Just behind the inspectors, Mr Tick could see the vase of perfect roses he'd noticed earlier. Only now they weren't perfect at all! His heart beat faster as he saw scattered petals and squashed stems on the floor. It looked as though someone had stamped on them!

'Those flaming kids! When I find out who has done this, I'll . . .' he growled under his breath. He rushed towards the flowers and scooped them up, but he slipped on some petals and skidded into the table, banging his shin. His eyes watered and his mouth opened in a silent 'o' of pain.

The inspectors turned towards him just as he stopped rubbing his shin and stood up straight. He smiled thinly and tucked the crumpled stems back into the vase.

'Ah, those children – such high spirits!' he laughed nervously. He shook his head and stuck a finger in his ear and wiggled it about inside. He could have sworn he'd heard a ghostly laugh

when he said 'high spirits'. He frowned slightly. *I must be working too hard* . . . he thought.

He held out his hand towards the inspectors. The woman looked at it and wrinkled her nose. She didn't like the idea of touching the finger

he'd just stuck into his ear. She pushed her colleague forwards.

'I'm Ms Morrison and this is Mr Willis.'

'I'm so very pleased to meet you! Welcome to our wonderful school!' Mr Tick gushed. He grabbed Mr Willis's hand and shook it enthusiastically. 'I trust you'll find everything shipshape and that you'll give us a glowing report!' he enthused.

The inspector looked at him gravely.

'I think *we* shall be the judges of that, Mr Tick. Time, as they say, will tell.' Mr Willis pushed his glasses up his nose with his finger. 'We should like to begin our inspection with the English Department, please.'

'Ah, yes! English. We study all the classics here, Mr Willis. *To Kill a Hummingbird* – such a favourite of mine! And *Lord of the Fleas* – such mastery! Shakespeare too – oh, yes!'

Ms Morrison looked startled.

'I think you'll find it's *Mockingbird* and *Flies* . . .' she said, frowning.

'Oh, no – you'll not find any nasty infestations of horrid little creatures here! Not unless you count the year sevens! Ha, ha!' said Mr Tick. His laughter choked to a halt as he saw the inspectors staring at him, unamused. 'Just my little joke! Our year sevens are, of course, a credit to the school . . .' he rubbed his damp palms on his suit. 'Ahem. Will you come this way?'

The inspectors stared at him for a moment, and Mr Willis noted something down on his clipboard.

'Lead on, Mr Tick . . .' he said, grimly.

'Ah, yes, leadership is something I take very seriously. Very seriously indeed, of course, what with being the headmaster,' Mr Tick babbled on. 'I am passionate about my job. I want people to look at St Sebastian's and say – Yes! There is a school with excellent leadership . . .'

Mr Willis sighed. It looked as though this was going to be one of *those* inspections.

CHAPTER 8
HANGING AROUND

James skidded to a halt in front of the changing-room doors.

'That was close!' he puffed. 'When that door slammed shut, I thought I was going to wet myself!'

'Well, at least you were in the right place!' joked Alexander. His cheeks were red with the effort of running to the gym block.

'For once, Stick, I'm glad to hear your terrible jokes!' laughed Lenny. 'We need all the laughs we can get at the moment!'

'Right – now we've caught our breath, it's time for gym!' said James, pushing the double doors open.

'Remember, Dad's really keen that we impress the inspectors with our special gym display,' said Alexander.

'Brrr . . .' shuddered Lenny. 'I just hope I can pull it off. I feel a bit wobbly after all that messing about in the toilets. It was awful!'

'You'll be fine, Lenny – come on!' James pulled on his gym shoes and hurled his clothes in a locker. He threw Lenny's gym shoes on the floor in front of his friend and helped Alexander find his shorts. 'Come on, come on, we're in a hurry – ready yet? Hup, hup, let's go!' He clapped his hands and mimed running on the spot. Alexander laughed.

'OK, OK – ready! I just hope the ghosts don't have any funny business planned for this visit from the inspectors!'

James rolled his eyes. 'No time to worry about that now – we've got a gym display to do!'

The boys piled into the gym and joined a line of pupils getting ready for the display. Ms Legg peered anxiously through the door every few minutes, watching out for the inspectors.

'We made it! Thank goodness – no inspectors yet!' smiled Alexander.

Ms Legg clapped her hands. 'Quick! They're coming! Everyone into their places!' Ms Legg grabbed shoulders, moving pupils around like giant chess pieces. 'I want you to be ready to start as soon as they arrive – come on!' Her voice cracked as she tried not to panic. She dived across the room and pressed the 'play' button on the CD player just as the inspectors pushed open the doors.

As the drum beats filled the room, James whispered, 'Here we go!' He gritted his teeth and ran towards the horse.

'Come on, Simpson, I know you can do it . . .' muttered Ms Legg under her breath.

James landed perfectly square on the springboard and leapt high into the air.

'Wonderful, James!' Ms Legg encouraged. 'You look as light as a . . .' The teacher's words tailed off as James soared over the horse, clearing it easily, but carried right on going! Suddenly, everywhere she looked, pupils were flinging themselves about the gym. And every time somebody jumped, they were propelled up into the air.

'Wow! It seems that the gym is a pocket of low gravity. I wonder if there were sunspots last night or –' mused Alexander.

'No time for that, professor! It's your turn!' Lenny hissed in his ear.

Alexander looked startled as Lenny pushed him forwards gently. Alexander ran, jumped – and shot into the air! His mouth split into an enormous grin.

This must be what astronauts feel when they are on the moon! he thought excitedly. He looked down and saw Lenny jump – and fly up to join him, floating around in the air.

'Welcome to the stratosphere, Lenny!' Alexander called.

Lenny's eyes were wide. He wriggled his fingers experimentally and spun in the air. 'Eh? Speak English, Stick!' he called back.

'Why did the boy become an astronaut?' asked Alexander, so happy he thought he'd celebrate with a joke.

James frowned and shrugged.

'Cos he was no earthly good!' cried Alexander.

James chuckled and started to swim through the air, chasing Lenny and Alexander. 'This is amazing!' he laughed. 'Got you!' James grabbed Alexander's ankle and they both spun in the air like a Frisbee. 'What do you make of all this?' he asked as they slowed down.

'Not sure – things are a bit up in the air at the moment!' Alexander grinned.

James rolled his eyes.

'Only you could be spinning around in mid air and still manage to crack a rotten joke like that!' he smiled.

The air was filled with pupils whirling, swimming and laughing. Ms Legg stared up at them, open-mouthed. *I don't remember this part of the display* . . . she thought.

'Look down there!' James pointed at the inspectors. They were staring up at the pupils floating past, pointing and giggling and poking each other in the ribs.

'Well, that's not very professional behaviour,' frowned Alexander. 'I don't think "pointing and laughing at pupils" is in *The School Inspectors' Handbook*!'

James raised his eyebrows. 'Only you, Stick, would comment on that when the rest of us are gobsmacked because we're floating round the gym. You really *do* take after your dad!'

Alexander looked pleased, even though his friend hadn't actually meant it as a compliment.

'Be fair though, James,' said Lenny. 'Look at them – I can see the woman's dandruff from here. Not only are they pointing and laughing at us, but she's turned up for work with hair like a mangy old cat.' He pointed at the inspectors, and Alexander looked closely.

'Wow! Is it just me, or can you see their auras, too?' said Alexander.

'*Auras*? Here we go again! Try and use words us mere mortals can understand, would you?' James suggested.

'Sorry,' Alexander shrugged. 'An aura is a glowing, coloured light shimmering around the outside edge of people, animals or plants that tells the observer about the health and nature of the –'

'Never mind that!' snapped James. 'The point is, they're glowing! What does that tell you?'

'Well,' said Alexander, 'according to scholars, it tells you they're strong willed . . .'

'FORGET THE AURAS!' shouted James. 'They're glowing because they're *ghosts*!'

'Sorry, James! I got a bit carried away there,' said Alexander. 'Hey – Why aren't ghosts good at telling lies?'

'Well, I don't know . . .' said Lenny.

'Because you can see right through them!'

James groaned. 'Stick! This is no time for jokes – we've seen this before. They're ghosts! Now, what are we going to do?'

'Look – they're leaving!' hissed Lenny. The In-Spectres were grinning and nodding to one another. The woman reached her hand up and waved her fingers slowly at James and Alexander. Her eyes flashed red as she mouthed 'Bye-bye!'

'That was *weird*!' James shuddered.

'James Simpson, master of understatement!' Alexander laughed nervously.

CHAPTER 9
FIRST IMPRESSIONS

Mr Tick took a deep breath and a slurp of his extra-strong, bitter coffee. He brushed down his already clean suit and gritted his teeth.

'Right, Miss Keys – back into battle!' he grinned. Miss Keys smiled. 'I need to find those inspectors and make sure they see how great I . . . ahem, *the school* is!'

'Good luck, sir – I know you can do it!' she simpered. She slipped a clothes brush out of the drawer and swept it over the headmaster's suit jacket.

Mr Tick smiled bravely and strode out of the office.

Now, where have they got to? he wondered to himself. *Could it be the science lab?* He paused and looked inside. Mr Watts was holding up a plastic model of a molecule. *Nope, no inspectors there. Perhaps they're in the design and technology room.* He caught sight of his reflection in the window and grew distracted. *Do I deserve a lovely new suit? Of course I do!* He was so busy smoothing down his lapels that he didn't see Mr Willis and Ms Morrison march past the end of the corridor.

Moments later, the In-Spectres drifted round the corner and stopped by the side of him. Mr Tick was so busy straightening his tie he failed to notice them. His nose twitched, then he screwed up his face.

'What *is* that appalling pong? Has Mr Wharpley *still* not sorted out those toilets? I'll have to see him about that . . .' he muttered.

He turned and jumped as he discovered the In-Spectres standing directly in front of him. He clutched his chest.

'Good lord! I didn't hear you creeping . . . I mean . . . goodness, it's hot in here, isn't it?'

He flapped a hand backwards and forwards in front of his face, then leant over and tried to open the nearest window. He tugged and heaved, but the window didn't budge.

'Of course, we have to keep these windows fastened for the pupils' safety. Security is a top priority in schools these days!'

With a sharp crack the window flew open, showering the In-Spectres with flakes of the old paint that had sealed it shut. Mr Tick brushed his suit off carefully.

'Ah – fresh air! That's better!' He grinned at the In-Spectres. They stared back, stony faced. Not a trace of a smile. The female In-Spectre stuck her hand out in front of her.

'Pleased to meet you,' she said, coldly.

Surely *they haven't forgotten me already!* thought Mr Tick. He gulped and fixed his smile as it slipped. He grabbed her hand and shook it.

'Oh! You're so cold! Perhaps I'd better close the window after all.'

He frowned, shaking his head in an attempt to clear it. A gust of wind swirled around his ankles,

causing his trouser legs to inflate so he looked like a clown. A jolt like an electric current shot up his arm, and he dropped the In-Spectre's hand. Had this crazy woman just used one of those joke-shop buzzers on him?

'What on earth?' he exclaimed, as he looked into the In-Spectre's eyes. They'd caught the dim light in the corridor and were reflecting silver light, like wolf eyes. Or could they be . . . *glowing*? Surely not! Mr Tick shuddered and stepped away from both In-Spectres. He closed the window and, in the reflection of the glass, he saw them staring at him. Their eyes glinted. His neck prickled and he rubbed it. He turned to face them.

'Ahem, yes, well, I'm sure you have places to go and people to see! I mustn't hold you up now!'

Mr Tick smiled nervously and stepped sideways, away from his visitors. Then he stepped sideways again, putting as much distance between himself and the spooky In-Spectres as possible.

'Erm, I have some very important paperwork to do now . . . Must dash! I'll see you later!'

He spun on his heel and rushed off towards his office. Rubbing his arm, he wondered exactly what was going on.

CHAPTER 10
AIR DISPLAY

In the gym, the pupils were still floating round in the air.

'We need to get down from here!' James called. 'Those ghosts are loose in the school! Who *knows* what they're up to!'

'Well, we could use the laws of equal and opposite attraction,' said Alexander, rubbing his chin.

'In English, professor?' sighed James.

'I mean, we could let our friend physics come to the rescue again! If we push off from the wall

bars, we can propel ourselves back down to the ground.'

'*Our friend physics*? It's no friend of mine!' laughed Lenny.

'Yup – we've seen your grades!' Alexander agreed. 'You know, it's quite nice up here, really. I feel like we're all planets. Hey, that reminds me of a joke – How does the barber cut the moon's hair?'

'Don't know,' shrugged James.

''e clips it!'

'Arrgh! Will you focus?' groaned James. 'Come on – we'll give your idea a try. What have we got to lose?' he said, diving towards the wall bars.

He grabbed Lenny's T-shirt on the way past and pulled him down. Alexander pushed himself towards the bars as best he could, but spun out of control.

'Heeelp! I'm going straight for the skylight!' he squeaked.

Lenny kicked off the wall bars again and swooped after Alexander.

'Hold on, I'm coming!' he called.

Lenny grabbed Alexander's ankle and they both turned in the air, drifting in a circle like a human snowflake.

'Well done, Lenny!' called James. 'If you push towards me I'll grab you as you pass.'

'OK, Stick, let's pretend we're swimming,' Lenny said.

He started to pull towards James, arm over arm in a sort of 'air crawl'.

'Erm, I've never been a very strong swimmer . . .' said Alexander.

He flapped around in circles for a bit, waving his arms and legs.

'Blimey!' laughed James as he grabbed his friend. 'You look like a fish!'

Alexander smiled brightly. 'Really? Well, that must be because I was trying to swim like a barracuda! They secrete slimy mucous from a gland under their skin – it reduces drag by sixty per cent, you know.'

'No – like a fish out of water!' quipped James. 'I must spend too much time with you – that was as bad as one of your jokes!'

James pulled Lenny's top and Lenny caught hold of Alexander again.

'This must be that teamwork Ms Legg is always going on about!' smiled Alexander.

Soon, the three friends had caught hold of the bars. They walked themselves to the ground hand over hand down them. As soon as they touched the floor they stopped floating.

'Ah! Madame Gravity reasserts her rule!' smiled Alexander.

'Yeah – and we're not floating either!' winked Lenny.

'But look up there – it looks like a film of the moon landings, zero gravity and all that!' said James.

'Actually, you only find zero gravity in deep space, not on the moon, James!' said Alexander.

James pushed his shoulder playfully.

'OK, OK. But look at them all up there!'

Pupils floated all round the gym. A small girl

turned a series of forward rolls giggling the whole time. Boys were playing 'air tag', chasing each other around the ceiling. One girl was blowing a shuttlecock through the air, like some kind of odd game of 'keepie-uppie'.

'Look! There's The Gorilla!' said James pointing.

The bully was reaching out towards the wall bars, but kept missing. His face was a deep red and he was sweating. He started to whimper as he spun out of control again and caught a foot in the basketball hoop. He hung upside down like a huge, lumpy fruit bat.

'That's a weird take on a slam dunk!' Alexander guffawed.

By now, Gordon was furious. He pulled himself up on the hoop. There was a straining, popping noise, and the rivets started to come away from the wall. Desperate, Gordon flung himself towards the ropes hanging from the ceiling. There was a ripping sound.

'That's torn it!' snorted Alexander.

'What's got into you?' asked James.

'Look!' said Alexander, almost too helpless with laughter to lift his arm and point. 'I know Ms Legg said she wanted a spectacular display, but I don't think she had *that* in mind!'

As James and Lenny looked up they saw a gaping hole in the back of Gordon's shorts. They'd torn on the rivets. A pair of teddy bear-patterned boxers could be seen poking through the hole.

'Nice pants, Gordon!' shouted James.

'Just wait until I get down from here!' the bully growled.

'Careful, James – he might hit you with his teddy!' laughed Alexander.

One by one, the pupils were gradually starting to float back to the floor.

'Come on, guys, we'd better get out of here before he comes down!' laughed Lenny, heading for the door.

He peered through the glass. No In-Spectres. They pushed through the double doors back into the boys' changing room and sat on a bench.

'OK – let's get things clear,' said James. 'Firstly, we were all magically floating round the ceiling. Totally weird. Secondly, those ghastly ghostly inspectors were *glowing*.'

'Well,' smiled Alexander, 'I know Dad said he wanted a glowing report, but I don't think *that's* what he had in mind!' he laughed, nervously. 'Seriously though – I saw it too. Those were definitely in*spectres*, not inspectors!'

'Yeah – and did you notice the horrible smell? That nasty, dead-rat whiff – like in the toilets. You could smell it, too, couldn't you?' asked Lenny.

'Yes, I definitely detected something. The scent molecules must have risen on the currents of warm air created by the gym display –' said Alexander.

'Do you think we can focus on what's important for a minute, Einstein? You know – what your dad would call *the key issues*?' James groaned. 'The weird glowing, the horrible smell, the way we were all floating around like helium balloons – it was something that the ghosts did, it *must* be.'

Alexander went pale as a thought suddenly dawned on him.

'You know what they're up to, don't you? They want to mess up the inspectors' visit! The *real* inspectors. That's why they're here! Oh, no – poor Dad! What can we do?'

'Don't worry, we'll just have to find a way to stop them!' said James, banging his fist into his hand. 'We know there are *real* inspectors in the school and we want them to go away with a good impression of St Sebastian's. Quite a challenge there, even without the ghosts on the prowl!' he smirked. 'We'll just have to follow the impostors around to make sure they don't spring any more spooky surprises. Come on – there's no time to waste!'

'But if we follow the In-Spectres around we'll be late for maths! Dad'll go mad if he sees us!' complained Alexander.

'We can't take any chances, Stick. Who knows what other surprises the ghosts have in store for the real inspectors? Your dad would be even more angry if they saw anything weird and the school got a bad report!' said James.

The friends were in the corridor outside the maths room. The real inspectors were heading upstairs to watch a drama lesson.

'I don't suppose the ghosts can cause too much trouble in a drama class,' said Lenny.

'No. It's the design and technology room I'm worried about. Can you imagine the damage that could be done with a bunch of possessed power tools?' shuddered Alexander.

'Or the art room. With all those craft knives and pairs of scissors. It could be horrific!' James said, shaking his head. 'You're right, Lenny, a drama class *should* be safe, but I think we should keep watch anyway.'

The boys followed the inspectors up the stairs and peered nervously through the glass panel in the door to the hall where the drama class was taking place. The inspectors sat to one side as a group of pupils set up props and scenery.

'Look – it's Leandra!' Lenny smiled, spotting his older sister. 'She's been practising this scene for weeks. Hmmm . . . can't imagine *why* they chose her to be an old hag!'

James and Alexander sniggered quietly, breaking the tension.

'Which play is it?' asked James.

The girls were heaving a giant plant pot cunningly disguised as a cauldron across the stage area.

'It's "The Scottish Play",' Alexander announced, drawing an imaginary sword and thrusting it at James.

'I don't care if it's Welsh, African or Chinese – what play is it?' grumbled James.

'It's *Macbeth*. Thespians – that's actors to you lot – call it "The Scottish Play" because it's supposed to be unlucky to say the real name out loud,' said Alexander.

'Thank you, Stick – as usual, the font of all knowledge,' said James.

Alexander beamed. 'There's only one problem though.'

'What?'

'You said the real name. I hope that doesn't bring bad luck while the inspectors are in there –' Alexander's hand flew to his mouth.

Leandra, her pretty best friend Stacey and their classmate Bethany were dressed in black cloaks and hats. The boys watched as the three girls began to stir the cauldron with their broomsticks. Leandra raised her arms dramatically in the air.

'Twice the brindled cat hath mew'd,' she cackled.

A terrible screech ripped through the air. It sounded like fingernails being scraped down a blackboard. Alexander jumped and clutched his chest.

'Crikey! Their special effects are good! That nearly gave me a cardiac arrest!' he panted.

'It had me going, too,' said Lenny. 'I think I know what it was – Leandra's been lurking in the garden at home for weeks now, recording the neighbourhood cats. She must have amplified their yowling through the speaker system.'

'Phew! So it was only *cat*erwauling, not a *cat*astrophe!' laughed Alexander, calming down.

James frowned.

'What is it?" asked Lenny.

His friend raised a shaking finger to point at the sound system. The plug wasn't in the socket.

'You mean the wail that sent me into orbit was *real*?' Alexander shivered.

'Let's not jump to conclusions. We need more evidence,' said James, firmly.

At that moment, clouds of thick green smoke belched from the cauldron. The girls started to choke and the inspectors wafted the smoke away with their clipboards. Leandra swiped at the smoke with her broomstick. She carried on regardless.

'What a professional!' whispered Alexander.

'Eye of newt . . .' Leandra recited. There was a wet squelch as a slimy, green newt-shaped object fell into the cauldron.

'. . . And toe of frog,' said Stacey, following Leandra's lead.

Something small, green and toe-shaped fell from above the stage and landed in the cauldron with a 'splat'.

'Wool of bat, and tongue of dog!' wailed Bethany, swirling her hands in front of her face mysteriously.

Her fingers became tangled in a small ball of fleece, and a wet, leathery tongue fell on to her hand and slid to the floor. It left a slimy, red trail.

'Somebody tell me those things were just part of the special effects,' whispered Alexander again.

'Looks like we have our evidence,' said James.

'Those things were real? *Gross!*' Lenny wrinkled his nose.

'Well, technically speaking, if they were conjured by the In-Spectres they're probably just gobbets of ectoplasmic matter, masquerading as . . .'

'Try telling Stacey they're just gobbets!' said James to Alexander.

Stacey was retching.

As they watched, spell ingredients showered down into the cauldron. A series of wet splats let everyone know that they were all too real.

Through the clouds of smoke, the boys could see the inspectors furiously scribbling notes on their clipboards.

'That's it – we're too late to stop them. The ghosts have won! What will Dad do now?' moaned Alexander, holding his head in his hands.

'It might still be OK. I'm sure we can do *something* to help,' said Lenny.

'No, that's it. St Sebastian's is going down the drain . . . or should I say the sewers . . .' groaned Alexander.

'Watch out! The In-Spectres are coming!' hissed James from the top of the staircase.

'I thought they were in the drama class, but there must be more of them than we realised!'

The ghostly In-Spectres were marching up the stairs towards them. A ghastly green glow lit up the walls as they passed.

'Quick! The real inspectors are getting ready to leave the drama class!' Lenny called. 'We've got to stop them all meeting, or the school's done for! Come on!'

'It's no use . . . all is lost!' Alexander moaned, covering his eyes with his arm.

'Snap out if it,' growled James, shaking Alexander's arm. 'Help me hold these doors shut!'

James and Lenny leant against the double doors so the inspectors couldn't push them open. Mr Willis's face appeared through the glass.

'Sorry, sir! The doors appear to be jammed!' smiled James. 'We're trying our best to get you out – never fear!'

Alexander sniffled, then blew his nose. He pushed his shoulders back and tapped his fingers against the side of his head.

James looked at him sideways. 'What *are* you doing? You can't crack up now! We need your help!'

'Huh? Oh – it helps me think – wait – I've got it!' he whooped. 'We use the concept of levers to stop them from opening the doors!'

Alexander pointed at his friends' feet.

'What *is* he on about?' James said to Lenny.

'I think he means we each need to jam a foot against the doors to stop the inspectors from opening them,' explained Lenny.

'Well, why didn't he just *say* so?' James rolled his eyes.

The glowing In-Spectres walked past them into the boys' toilet. They looked straight ahead and didn't even seem to notice the boys.

'I think we're safe!' hissed Lenny.

'Right – after three, let go,' said James. 'One . . . two . . . three!' said James.

The real inspectors tumbled out of the drama hall.

'I'm so terribly sorry!' mumbled Alexander.

'The doors were jammed! They've just been replaced and they tend to stick,' James explained, smoothly. 'The headmaster is terribly keen on keeping the school up to date and well decorated! Sorry for any inconvenience!'

Mr Willis's mouth opened and closed like a goldfish.

'That was ridiculous!' he blustered. 'If you had just kept out of the way, we would have been able to get out. We're far too busy for nonsense like this!' he grumbled, brushing his hair out of his eyes and pulling himself together. 'Now, run along! Don't you have a class to go to?'

'Sorry, sir!' James said, hustling Alexander and Lenny away.

Ms Morrison brushed her skirt smooth and wisps of green smoke coiled off her. 'Most odd . . . quite an experience . . .' she mumbled.

'Repulsive props. I blame all those computer games myself,' said Mr Willis. 'Incredibly . . . erm . . . realistic stuff.'

He made a quick note on his clipboard.

CHAPTER 12
BITTERSWEET VICTORY

'That was priceless! My plan's done the trick!' Edith gushed to Ambrose as they paused inside the boys' toilets before heading back down to the sewer. 'What a wonderful idea to make all those ingredients fall out of the air. Credit where it's due though, I must commend Bertram. He was superb!'

Smug old hag, thought Ambrose to himself. 'Yes, Edith,' he agreed out loud.

'Those silly inspectors must have been horrified!' she ranted on. 'Oh, I do wish we could

have been inside with them to enjoy it properly instead of wasting our precious energy levitating so we could see through the window! Mind you, it was worth it. Perhaps the school will even get a visit from a witch finder after all that. Those girls could be had up for casting spells – now wouldn't that be wonderful? Nothing like a good old witch ducking . . .'

Edith went misty-eyed at the very thought.

'Come on, let's peep around the door and watch those inspectors run away screaming!' she cackled, pulling Ambrose by the arm.

They watched the inspectors walk past the door and down the staircase, their heads together.

'Well, they're not screaming,' said Edith, her head on one side. 'That's a bit disappointing . . . but they're definitely plotting something! I'm willing to bet it's the closure of the school – no more St Sebastian's, eh, Ambrose? What

a wonderful thought! The downfall of an entire school – down to Edith Codd, woman of action!' She let out a victorious cackle. 'Come along, Ambrose, time to go back down to the sewer – in triumph!'

Ambrose sighed. Edith spun round at the sound and Ambrose pasted the most convincing smile he could manage on to his face.

'I think we should have a ball in the amphitheatre to celebrate my, ahem, *our* success! I'm sure Lady Grimes would approve! Let's have some decorations – how about cobweb festoons? – and we could have snacks –'

Ambrose's head snapped up. Snacks? He liked the sound of that. He rummaged around in his pouch looking for his leech tin. He popped off the lid and chose a fat leech from a knot of writhing black bodies.

'Down the hatch!' he chuckled. There was nothing like a good juicy leech to cheer him up.

William was hanging round the school library, feeling miserable. It was one of his favourite places. He couldn't read, but he loved to stroke the books and imagine the knowledge they contained. In his daydreams, he sat with James, Lenny and Alexander, reading at one of the big library tables.

'That'll never happen now . . .' he sighed to himself. 'I can't bear to even think about life without the school and my friends . . .'

A sob caught in his throat.

'Cheer up, young man!' smiled Lady Grimes. 'I'm sure it won't be as bad as all that! You still have Ambrose and me. We'll look after you!'

William tried to smile. He liked Lady Grimes, but he still felt crushed by the idea of life without the pupils of St Sebastian's. They made the afterlife worth living.

The librarian, Ms Byron, was slowly picking up all the books that had mysteriously been thrown about the room. The floor was covered in great heaps of books, magazines and papers. One minute she'd had her head down at her desk, happily cataloguing books, the next she'd heard a noise like a gust of wind followed by a series of thumping noises. Putting down her coffee, she'd looked up to see books tumbling off the shelves.

An earthquake? In Grimesford? she'd wondered.

Once the books stopped falling, she'd rushed to the geography section and started researching the possibility of earthquakes in the region. Unfortunately, the geography section was no longer anywhere to be seen, hidden under a heap of thick history books.

Strange . . . Ms Byron had thought to herself. *They're shelved on the opposite side of the room. Spooky . . . Could it be some sort of supernatural*

happening? Or a black hole opening? No, too far-fetched. Silly old me! Things like that just don't happen in Grimesford! Oh, well, better get on!

By the time she'd dug out the books she wanted and finished her research, her coffee was cold. She was daydreaming about the book she

would one day write about her amazing experiences as a librarian.

I've always rather seen myself as an action hero . . . she thought. She patted her sensible cotton slacks and imagined they were army trousers with a utility belt. She picked up a window pole and brandished it about her like a lance.

Library Raider – *I can see it now! Saving books from certain destruction . . .*

Ms Byron was so lost in her daydream that she didn't notice the books apparently floating back on to the shelves of their own accord. An invisible William was brushing them off carefully and replacing them one by one.

'No more St Sebastian's. I'd die of a broken heart if I wasn't dead already . . .' he sighed to himself as he worked. 'No more James, no more Lenny, no more Alexander,' he cried softly. 'Nowhere to get away from awful Edith, no fun, no friends . . .'

Then a horrible thought struck him and his hand flew to his mouth.

'No more Stacey! Oh, my afterlife is over!' he sobbed out loud.

CHAPTER 13
RED-LETTER DAY

Mr Tick bobbed his head happily and sang himself a little ditty as he played another game of solitaire on the computer in his office. Or 'attending to important paperwork', as he called it.

Miss Keys knocked and entered, bringing in a pile of letters.

'Ah, Miss Keys. I hope you're having a morning as glorious as your good self!' he grinned.

Miss Keys flushed pink and giggled.

'Lovely, thank you, sir. Shall I pop the coffee-maker on?'

'Wonderful idea . . . super . . . marvellous . . .'

Mr Tick wasn't really listening. He was too busy admiring his reflection in the silver letter opener Miss Keys had given him for Christmas last year.

'Oh, you handsome devil!' he whispered to himself under his breath. He rubbed his fingertips over the engraving of his initials. 'Richard Anthony Tick . . . such an imposing name really, when you think about it . . .' he sighed.

He sat up straight in his chair, feeling terribly important.

'Hmmm . . . what have we here? An education catalogue – bin it; an invitation to the headmasters' conference – yawn; an application for a place – that means more money . . . there's one for you to sort out,' he said, handing the letter to Miss Keys. 'Ooh! *Solitaire Monthly*! Excellent! I've been waiting for this. They run profiles on important players, so pretty soon it's

bound to be yours truly smiling up from the features page. I sent them a photo, you know, the one I always send out with my Christmas cards.'

Miss Keys knew only too well. She kept it in a shiny, silver frame beside her bed.

Mr Tick picked up the magazine and a heavy, important-looking letter fell into his lap. The envelope was thick and had 'Department of Inspection – Education Division' embossed across the top.

'Good lord! That was quick!' He fumbled and dropped the envelope on the floor.

Miss Keys rushed to pick it up. They bumped heads under his desk. Mr Tick snatched the letter from her with shaking hands.

'This is it, Miss Keys! The report from the inspectors . . .' he slashed at the envelope with the letter opener, as though he was slaying a particularly fierce dragon. He put the envelope down on the table and poked it with a pencil.

Then he picked it up again, shook it and held it up to the light. Finally, he ripped it open and read the letter.

'Satisfactory! *Wonderful!* Miss Keys – our school is generally satisfactory!' Mr Tick jumped up, clutching the paper. He read on.

'They loved the drama and PE departments – excellent! And I quote, "The dramatic scene from *Macbeth* showed dedication from all concerned – teachers, actors and backstage technicians. Special mention should be made of the wonderful but gruesome props. These were so realistic that they reflect upon the excellence that must also exist in the art department." I always knew it, of course. This is *fabulous* news!'

He grabbed Miss Keys and plonked a kiss on her cheek. She put her hand to her face and looked at him, starry-eyed.

I'll never wash that cheek again. Oh, be still my beating heart . . . she thought.

Mr Tick grabbed her hands and danced her round the room, laughing and skipping.

The headmaster read on. '"The gymnastics display was first rate. The pupils showed great enthusiasm and a lightness of foot that could be

said to defy gravity"!' He grinned. 'I must tell the whole school . . . the whole of Grimesford . . . the world!' He threw back his head and laughed. 'Miss Keys, get the *Grimesford Journal* on the phone and tell them we have great news – front-page news!' He bounced out of the office, carrying the letter and a drawing pin.

I'll start with the noticeboard and then call a meeting in the staffroom . . . or the hall . . . he thought.

James, Lenny and Alexander were in the corridor, on their way to double history.

'Look, Stick – it's your dad!' said James, pointing at Mr Tick as he pinned something to the noticeboard. 'Do you think he knows anything yet?'

Mr Tick straightened his tie and walked off smiling towards the staffroom. There was a definite spring in his step.

'Well, it's not like Dad to tidy up noticeboards around school, so I think there's a good chance!'

Alexander said, frowning. 'But I don't know if I want to read it. If the school's closing down because of an awful report, Dad will lose his job and we'll have to move away . . .'

'It might not be *that* bad,' said Lenny, putting his arm round Alexander's shoulder. 'We did everything we could to help. We gave it our best shot . . .'

'Well, we have to go and look – it's the only way to find out,' said James. 'Come on – let's see what it says.'

Alexander trudged towards the noticeboard like a man on his way to his own execution. He took a deep breath and looked for the letter. He saw a notice about healthy eating featuring a smug-looking dancing orange and another about what to do if you found an infestation of head lice, but no letter.

'Where is it? Where is it?' he panicked, scrabbling at the sheets of paper wildly.

'Steady on!' James said gently. 'Look – there it is!' He pointed at a crisp piece of paper at the top of the board.

Alexander peered at it and laughed. 'It says . . . it says . . . the school is satisfactory!' he shouted.

'Well – that's a matter of opinion . . .' muttered James. He grinned, unable to tease his friend any longer. 'That means we are stuck with you *forever* then!'

He groaned, clutching at his throat and gurgling.

The friends ran off down the corridor, laughing and high-fiving each other.

Irritated by the noise, Mr Wharpley stomped up from his room in the cellar to see what all the fuss was about.

'What's going on? Noisy kids! What have they got to be so happy about?' he muttered to himself. 'If the school closes and they have to travel in all weathers to the other one across

town they'll not be so happy – and I'll be out of a job.'

He saw a new sheet of paper pinned to the top of the noticeboard.

'What's this? If those kids have been pinning rude cartoons of me on the board again, I'll . . .' he grumbled.

He reached up to tear the drawing down and saw it was a letter from the inspectors.

'Satisfactory? That means OK – the school isn't closing!' Mr Wharpley muttered to himself. 'I have a job, I have a job!' he shouted to the empty corridor. He wiggled his hips happily, giving a little Elvis sneer. He swung his arm in a wheel around his head and grabbed an imaginary microphone. 'U-huh . . . I have a job . . . U-huh-huh . . . I am the king!'

'Of course,' he said, pulling himself together, 'a good report just means more flaming pupils wanting places here, and that means more

mess . . .' He made his way back down the stairs, grumbling to himself.

The letter fluttered as a breeze swept across the noticeboard. William had been moping along the corridor, saying goodbye to all the places and people he would miss when the school closed down. Edith had ruined everything.

Now, William couldn't read – but he could hear. And he could hardly believe his ears! He'd overheard Mr Wharpley talking to himself – the inspectors had liked the school after all! So now St Sebastian's was safe! His friends would be staying! He swirled into the air with excitement and floated up towards the ceiling, carried on a cloud of happiness. He touched a light bulb that Reg had been meaning to replace for weeks and it flared into life. Fizzing with excitement, William turned victory rolls in the air.

I must tell Ambrose! he thought. *And Edith!* He grinned as he shot off back to the sewers.

Edith was in the amphitheatre, rearranging her collection of hairpins. They were actually the plastic clips that held blocks of freshener in the toilet bowls, but Edith didn't know that. She thought she'd use them to pin up her hair.

'School's out, for*ever*!' Edith sang happily. She'd heard the song once on Mr Wharpley's music box in his room and had always thought it was a charming ditty. That singer – Alice, the box-voice had called her – had a very deep voice for a girl though. She shook her head. 'These modern girls . . . dear me . . .' she grumbled to herself.

'Ahem, Edith?' William said politely.

Edith flew up in the air and snagged some ectoplasm on a rock jutting out of the wall. She settled back to earth leaving a piece of her arm dangling from the wall.

'William! I was doing something terribly important! Why have you disturbed me?' she screeched.

William smiled sweetly. 'I was up in the school and heard the pupils talking –'

'Were they packing up their silly little school bags, weeping and wailing? Ahhh, I almost feel sorry for them – *not*!' she roared with laughter.

'Erm, no, they were laughing, in fact.'

'*Laughing*?' asked Edith, spinning round to face William. A frown was beginning to appear on her wrinkled face. 'Insane, broken, hysterical laughter?'

'Happy laughter, actually,' William smiled again. He just couldn't help himself. The smiles kept leaking out.

'They must be happy because their crummy dump of a school is closing down and they never have to set foot in it again,' decided Edith.

'No, a letter made them happy,' smiled William.

'A letter? Why? What did it say?' Edith was advancing on William, menacingly.

He stepped back. 'They said the school was "satisfactory" and that it wasn't closing!' he said, moving his hands slowly to cover his ears in preparation for her reaction.

'*Not closing*?' Edith shrieked. 'After all my work – *not closing*!' She threw herself furiously about the amphitheatre, kicking rats and stamping on spiders. 'It's not fair! I can't *bear* it!'

Bertram Ruttle stepped forwards with his bone xylophone.

'I know, Edith, I'll play a happy little tune to cheer you up!' He started to play a jig.

Edith tore the xylophone from his hands and threw it to the ground, where it smashed into pieces.

'Shut up, you stupid little man!' she screamed, and stormed off into a corner to torment an elderly ghost to cheer herself up.

'Oh, Bertram – I'm so sorry!' said William.

'Not to worry, lad. It was only my twelfth best xylophone – plenty more where that came from!' And he trundled off, humming happily.

William looked at Edith. She was spitting and shrieking. Every time she paused to take a breath, he heard the reassuring sound of school life going on overhead. He smiled and went in search of Ambrose. He'd be delighted. Lady Grimes, too.

Edith pointed a shaking finger at the roof.

'You may have won this time, but I'll be back!' she yelled.

Windows rattled all over the school. Miss Keys watched the coffee on her desk curiously. Circles and ripples appeared on the surface.

'Oh! That's just like in that film about dinosaurs, when the T. rex is coming . . . I hope nothing nasty's on its way!' she laughed to herself, nervously. 'Mind you, while Mr Tick's

in his office and there are choccy biscuits in the tin, all's well with my world!'

She settled back down to drink her coffee and read her exciting new book, *The Art of Being a Great Secretary*.

Back in the sewer, Edith Codd finally slumped down on to a pile of sacking, quite exhausted. A rat squeaked and pushed its way out of the folds. It gave Edith a hard stare and scuttled off. She sat up, irritably.

'Rat bite you, missus?' asked a passing ghost.

Ignoring him, Edith raised her fist in the air and shook it at the school overhead. 'Think you've won, do you? Pah! I'll prove that you can't keep a good ghost down. I'll soon find a way to finish St Sebastian's *forever*!' she threatened.

SURNAME: Scroggins

FIRST NAME: William

AGE: 667

HEIGHT: 1.4 metres

EYES: Pale blue with purple circles underneath

HAIR: Too mucky to tell really

FACT FILE

LIKES: Playing medieval football, gliding through walls, spying on Mr Tick's magic glowing box, pretending he's at school, protecting St Sebastian's

DISLIKES: Edith shouting at him; accidentally scaring people above ground; having to climb through a loo all the time; too much hard work

SPECIAL SKILL: Fooling people into thinking he's Alexander because he looks so much like him

INTERESTING FACT: William never went to school. He worked on his parents' farm from the age of six and was killed by the plague just five years later

For more facts on William Scroggins, go to **www.too-ghoul.com**

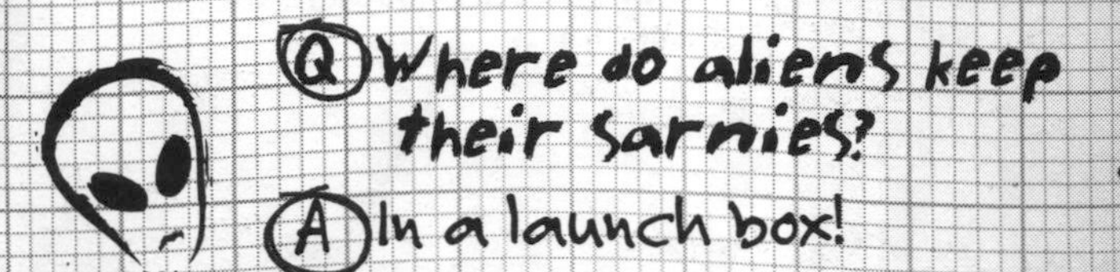

Q What do you call a vampire that lives in the kitchen?

A Spatula!

Knock knock

Who's there?

Emma . . .

Emma who?

Emma bit cold out here, will you let me in?

NOTE TO SELF: input these into jokes database at earliest convenience

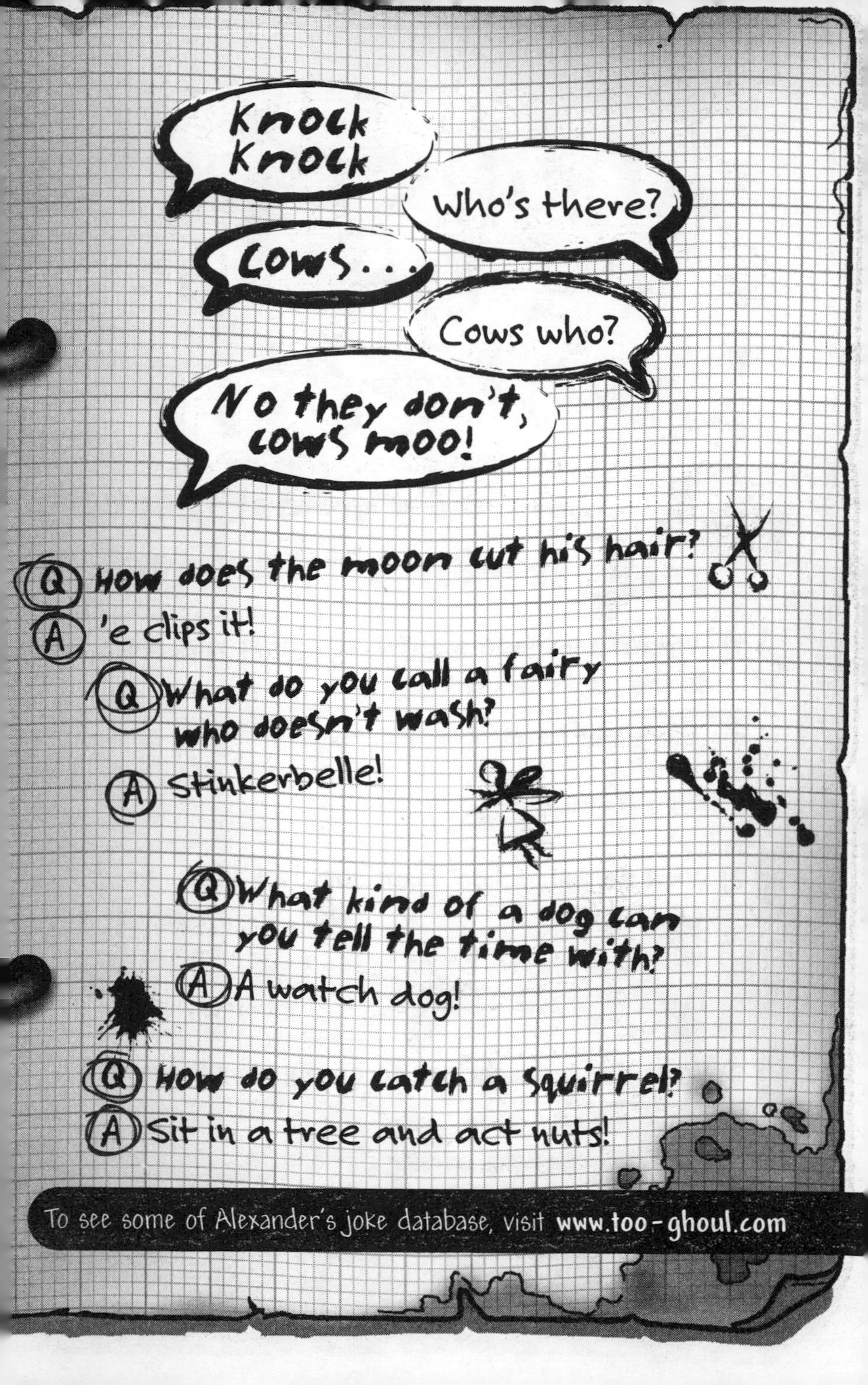

Knock Knock
Who's there?
Cows...
Cows who?
No they don't, cows moo!
Q How does the moon cut his hair?
A 'e clips it!
Q What do you call a fairy who doesn't wash?
A Stinkerbelle!
Q What kind of a dog can you tell the time with?
A A watch dog!
Q How do you catch a squirrel?
A Sit in a tree and act nuts!
To see some of Alexander's joke database, visit www.too-ghoul.com

Inspector OR In-Spectre?

Find out what your school inspector <u>really</u> is with this easy quiz!

1) When the inspectors arrive at your school, how do the pupils behave?

a. There's even more rioting than usual
b. Everyone is on their best behaviour
c. Pupils start levitating

2) What do your school inspectors look like?

a. Smart but rather angry
b. Clean, neat and very boring
c. They glow and have luminous red eyes

3) What do the inspectors do during your lessons?

a. Frown and shake their heads
b. Nod and make notes on their clipboards
c. Float above the ground and make howling noises

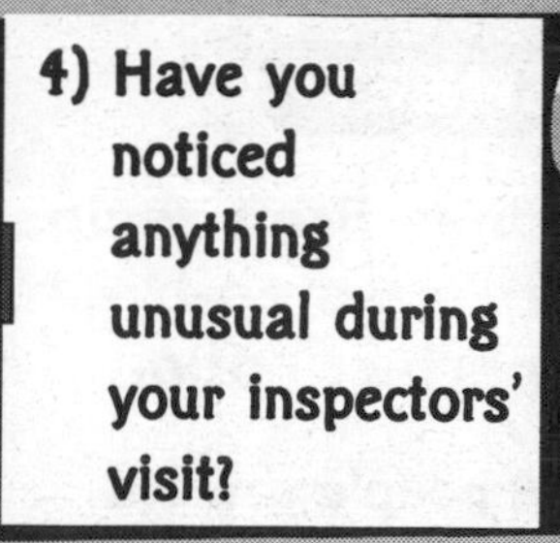

4) Have you noticed anything unusual during your inspectors' visit?

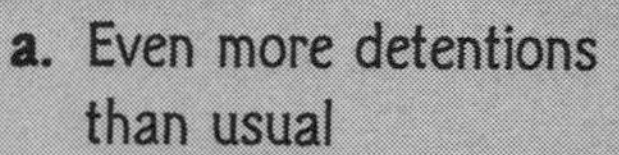

a. Even more detentions than usual
b. The teachers are suspiciously nice for once
c. There is a cloud of foul-smelling gas wafting round your school

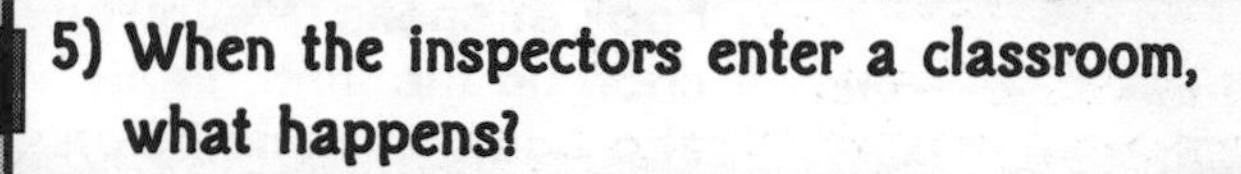

5) When the inspectors enter a classroom, what happens?

a. Nothing. The teacher's hiding under her desk anyway
b. Suddenly everyone's quiet and very well behaved
c. An icy wind blows through the room and it goes dark outside

How did you score?

Mostly As: Your inspectors aren't ghosts. But they are going to fail your terrible school!

Mostly Bs: You have normal school inspectors. But watch out for any glowing …

Mostly Cs: I'd steer clear of drama class if I were you. There are ghosts in your school **RIGHT NOW!**

Saturday Witchin'

RECIPE FACT SHEET

In case you missed that Witches Brew recipe from this morning's show, here's a step-by-step guide to cooking up the perfect potion

YOU WILL NEED:

1 large cauldron

An open fire

3 witches and a book of deadly spells

1 toad

1 newt's eye

2 frog's toes (frozen will do)

1 dog's tongue

1 wolf's tooth

1 lizard's leg

Remember, if you are casting spells on more than 6 people you will need to double the number of newts' eyes and frogs' toes.

INSTRUCTIONS:

1. Boil up your cauldron and start reciting hideous enchantments from your book of spells. Meanwhile, chop up the ingredients and add them one by one, making sure that the newt's eyes and lizard's legs don't stick to the side of the cauldron.

2. Stir slowly, while continuing to chant. You will know when your brew is ready when a thick, poisonous smoke fills the room and people nearby start to faint and retch. Serve piping hot.

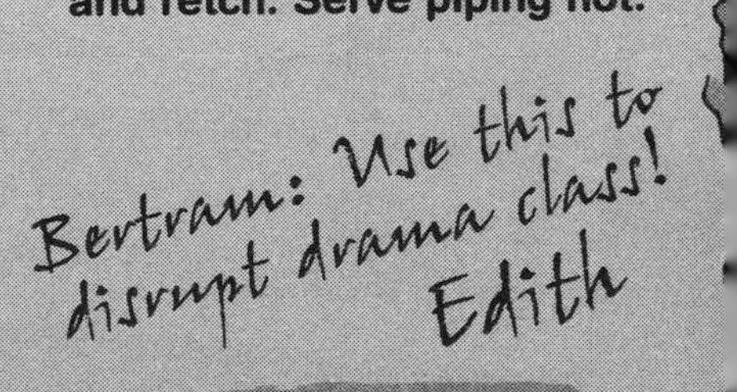

Can't wait for the next book in the series?

Here's a sneak preview of

SCHOOL SPOOKS DAY

available now from all good bookshops,

or **www.too-ghoul.com**

ELVIS PRESLEY

The American singer Elvis Presley is mentioned quite a few times in *School Spooks Day* (Mr Wharpley, the school caretaker, has a huge collection of his records).

Here are some interesting facts about Elvis:

- He was born in 1935 and died in 1977
- He is often called 'The King of Rock 'n' Roll'!
- He wiggled his hips when he was singing – older people thought this was disgusting!
- He once shot a TV set with a gun because he didn't like the show that was on!
- He was one of the most famous performers of the twentieth century, and is reported to have sold over one billion singles and albums, which would make him the biggest-selling solo artist of all time!

CHAPTER 1
SWAMPED

'U-huh-huh,' crooned Mr Wharpley, caretaker of St Sebastian's School, and owner of the world's greasiest hairstyle. He'd tried to shape it into an Elvis-style quiff, but the gunk from the school kitchen's deep-fat fryer just didn't work as well as real hair gel, and his fringe flopped about like a dead rat.

Picturing himself as his hero, Mr Wharpley spun the mop around to use it as a microphone but mistimed the move and slapped himself in the face with the sopping wet sponge.

Spluttering, he quickly looked around the changing rooms of the school's indoor swimming pool to make sure no one had seen the incident. Certain that he was alone, he whipped a master key from his shirt pocket, used it to open a nearby locker, and grabbed the clean trunks of a year-eight boy to dry his face.

Slamming the locker closed, Mr Wharpley spun the volume control of his ancient CD player as 'Hound Dog', his favourite Elvis tune of all time, began to ring out. He sang along, gyrating his hips in a way he believed made him look like The King of Rock 'n' Roll but, in reality, gave the impression that his underwear was full of itching powder.

Suddenly, there was a loud clanking sound, followed by a grating of metal on metal that set the caretaker's teeth on edge.

'What *now*?' he moaned, using the handle of his mop to switch off Elvis. He went in the

direction of the pool, taking care to avoid the footbath as he left the changing room. No point cleaning his boots twice in one month.

Mr Wharpley stood at the side of the swimming pool and gazed into the water. Something wasn't right, but he couldn't quite put his finger on it. The water was clean, the broken tiles had been repaired, and the swimming lanes had been repainted on the bottom with paint he was almost certain wouldn't be poisonous if swallowed. The water looked perfectly clear and still.

Perfectly clear and still. That was it. The flippin' pool filter had packed up! It was supposed to constantly drain whatever mess the little brats left in there and churn out clean water to replace it, but it had stopped.

The caretaker shuffled around the edge of the pool to the machine room on the far side. 'Make sure everything's ready for school sports day,

Mr Wharpley!' he whined, imitating the headmaster, Mr Tick. 'Everything has to be perfect for when the parents arrive!'

'The only way this school will be perfect is if we get rid of the little monsters that make my life a misery every day!' Mr Wharpley allowed himself a little smile at the wondrous thought of a school with no pupils as he searched his pockets for the key to the machine room.

Unlocking the door and tugging it open, he stared in horror at the mess in front of him. A metal lifesaving pole had fallen from its place on the wall and jammed in the cogs of the ancient pool filter. Despite clear instructions from health and safety that the lifesaving equipment needed to be available at all times, Mr Wharpley kept it all locked safely away in the machine room. He was now beginning to regret the decision.

Grabbing the handle, he tried to pull the pole free of the machine into which it was jammed.

It wouldn't move. Perhaps if he pressed his foot against the side of the filter to get a better grip? The elderly man raised a dirty boot and pushed hard while yanking at the pole. Yes! . . . The cogs were starting to turn.

In one swift movement, Mr Wharpley's foot slipped off the side of the filter and swung upwards, whereupon the turn-ups of his right trouser leg became caught in the machinery along with the pole.

'Oh, great!' groaned the caretaker, hopping on his free foot to try and stay upright. He let go of the pole with one hand and stretched out to try and free his leg. These trousers were only twelve years old, he had to be careful not to rip them.

Suddenly, the cogs jerked forwards a little more, snagging the left sleeve of his shirt in their teeth, along with the pole and his trousers.

'Oh, for flip's sake!' yelled Mr Wharpley. He would never live it down if anyone came in and

found him like this. He had to escape from the clutches of the pool filter.

With his free hand, the caretaker gripped the largest of the cogs and tried to turn it. The metal

teeth bit into his fingers as he slowly . . . ever so slowly . . . began to spin the cog around . . .

That was when the foot he was balancing on slipped from underneath him and Mr Wharpley spun upside down. His favourite tie – the one with the orange and brown spanner print on it – caught in between the cogs and pulled tight as the caretaker fell to the floor.

'Kkkxxggghhh!' gurgled the angry caretaker as the tie threatened to cut off his air supply. He . . . had . . . to . . . free . . . himself . . .

There was only one option left open: switch the filter to reverse. That way, he would have a second or so to pull his shirt, trousers and tie clear of the machinery as the cogs began to turn the opposite way. The problem was, he couldn't reach the lever with his one free arm. That just left his mouth.

Gripping the handle between his teeth – and cursing himself for buying such foul-tasting polish

– Mr Wharpley pulled down hard on the lever. It had been years since the filter had been run in reverse, and the handle was rusted in place. The caretaker gripped tight and pulled even harder.

The lever didn't move for a few seconds. Then, suddenly, it slammed into the reverse position, sending the cogs of the filter spinning in the opposite direction.

Mr Wharpley's trousers, shirt and tie came free and he fell backwards, grabbing for the handle of the pool pole. The pole came free of the cogs and fell away from the machine as the caretaker was catapulted backwards through the machine-room door and into the swimming pool with a splash.

Spluttering, Mr Wharpley made it back to the surface of the water just in time to see generations of slime, hair and sticking plasters come belching out of the grilles around the edges of the pool. Within seconds, the caretaker was swimming in what appeared to be a swamp

filled with dead skin, scabs, rotting earplugs and old toenails.

Mr Wharpley spat out a mouldy verruca sock and shuddered as he paddled wildly to stay above the now crusty surface of the pool.

Elvis had never gone through anything like this.